"Blushing suits you, Sara.

"It'll look a whole lot better when my skin's not this pasty white colour."

Leo clicked his tongue. "A woman like you should be sophisticated enough to accept compliments with better grace."

"Sorry, but I don't take orders from a guy who looks like a pirate." She lolled back against the rail. It felt good to let the sun pour over her body. "Stop laughing, Leo."

"If I'm a pirate, then the sea should be my only mistress. Is that what you want?"

Praise for Christina Hollis

"Christina Hollis is a terrific writer who creates likeable characters readers take to their hearts..."
~Nas Dean, Romance Book Paradise

His Majesty's Secret Passion

by

Christina Hollis

Millionaire's Club Series

This is a work of fiction. Names, characters, places, and incidents are either the product of the author's imagination or are used fictitiously, and any resemblance to actual persons living or dead, business establishments, events, or locales, is entirely coincidental.

His Majesty's Secret Passion

COPYRIGHT © 2015 by Christina Hollis

All rights reserved. No part of this book may be used or reproduced in any manner whatsoever without written permission of the author or The Wild Rose Press, Inc. except in the case of brief quotations embodied in critical articles or reviews.
Contact Information: info@thewildrosepress.com

Cover Art by *Debbie Taylor*

The Wild Rose Press, Inc.
PO Box 708
Adams Basin, NY 14410-0708
Visit us at www.thewildrosepress.com

Publishing History
First Champagne Rose Edition, 2015
Print ISBN 978-1-62830-753-5
Digital ISBN 978-1-62830-754-2

Millionaire's Club Series
Published in the United States of America

Dedication

To Martyn,
who makes all my dreams come true.

Chapter One

It's not every day James Bond swims right underneath you.

The experience propelled Sara out of the water like a missile. It wasn't 007 who met her on splashdown, but he was a water-slicked vision all the same. His perfect teeth, bronzed skin, and flashing dark eyes almost made up for giving her the fright of her life—but not quite.

With the sapphire Aegean Sea attacking her like CPR, Sara didn't have enough breath left for tact. "What the hell do you think you're doing?"

"You screamed, so I dived in." His voice lilted with a European accent Sara couldn't recognize.

The stranger lifted his arm to point at the crag high above. Water gushed from the sleeve of his sodden white shirt. Dragging the cuff across his face, he blinked the last droplets from his lashes. Long, thick black lashes.

Sara cursed herself silently. Surging hormones weren't to be trusted. They'd dragged her out of her depth before.

Her toes brushed sand. With a few frantic strokes toward the shore, she found her feet and waded up the beach. "You mean you saw blood in the water, and made like a shark." She winced as salty breakers licked the gash on her shin.

"Blood?"

"Something bit me." She bent to check the wound. There were no tooth marks on her leg, only a long jagged cut. She felt a blush spread like her bruises. Fancy thinking she was being attacked by a man-eating shark, in the privacy of a place like the Paradise Hotel! Late-night TV had a lot to answer for.

"That's unlikely. A rocky outcrop runs under the mouth of this cove. You probably scraped against it." Her self-appointed rescuer studied her legs with interest. "You'll live."

Sara dug her toes into the sand. "Rock or shark bite, it's still pretty painful."

He gave her a calculating look. "The way you screamed, I suppose *Jaws* was on television again last night."

She avoided his gaze. "I have no idea. There should be warning notices around here, telling people to take care."

"They're pinned up inside the summer house." He nodded toward a building at the head of the beach.

"Then there should be warning flags out here too."

"Why? This inlet is safe enough. There's a good depth of water at high tide. You got too close to the rocks, and the swell did the rest."

His sodden, transparent shirt clung to his muscles. They were rock hard. Sara wondered about the other parts of his body. If there was a Mr. Wet Tux competition, this guy would win it hands down.

Her thoughts revealed themselves in a smile. It got wider at the sight of his disapproval.

The points of Sara's nipples pushed against the thin fabric of her bikini top. She told herself it wasn't a reaction to this gorgeous guy. It must be the effect of cooling breezes on wet skin. She started some warm-down exercises as a distraction. Then she noticed the effect her stretches were having on him.

Casually, he dropped his hands in front of him like a professional soccer player facing a penalty. "I haven't noticed any of Nick's guests swimming out here before. Until now."

"Oh, come on! Everyone staying at the spa must love this beautiful bay." Sara straightened up, looking around at the cliffs. Rising from cleaned and sifted golden sand they towered against a clear blue sky.

"Lounging on the beach or swimming in the sea would get the paparazzi circling. The people who come here are trying to get away from it all. Calling it a spa lets them pretend they're here on doctors' orders."

Sara groaned. "Tell me about it! Relaxing is for people with time on their hands. That's what I told my doctor. But he still made me take this break."

The stranger had been sizing her up, but stopped. "You must have a heart of stone not to appreciate staying in a place like this."

"You aren't the first person to say something like that. I'm just not keen on enforced idleness. And far too many people think they know what's best for me."

"You didn't look to be idling. You were swimming like there really was a shark after you. The only exercise most of the guests take here involves lifting cutlery and glassware. I've never seen anyone in the water before."

"You saw me."

"You're pretty unmissable." His dark chocolate eyes were penetrating.

Unsettled, Sara tried to laugh. "Oh, please! I'm sure a charmer like you can do better than that, Sir Galahad!" The intensity of his gaze softened as she spoke, but he didn't smile. Not yet.

"My name's Leo, not Galahad. Leo Gregoryan," was all he said.

"It was a joke, Leo Gregoryan." She hesitated, but in spite of his words he didn't have the air of a man trying his luck. "I'm Sara Astley." She planted her hands on her hips, waiting for him to say something more.

He didn't. With time to think, she wondered if his surname rang a bell. She tipped her head on one side, and eyed him. "Should I know you?"

"I hope not. Nick assured me his spa is reserved for those who are keen to spend time away from the public eye. I want to make the most of my freedom while I still can."

His face was unforgettable, but that didn't help Sara place him. "Well, I'm sorry, Mr Gregoryan, but in my line of work I don't have time to watch TV. I've met a number of celebrities, though, and I haven't liked any of them."

"Good for you."

"You dived fully clothed off a rock, and you're saying it wasn't a publicity stunt?"

"Correct. I don't like celebrities either. There's a world of difference between tellystocracy and true aristocracy."

His charm was effortless. That made puncturing it irresistible for Sara. "I assumed you'd done it on the excuse of making an online splash."

"No, I did it because I thought you were in trouble.

I'd been watching you from the terrace. That was much more interesting than yet another champagne reception."

"Ah." Sara nodded. "That explains your clothes. I thought only bridegrooms wore monkey suits at eleven o'clock in the morning."

He grinned, flexing like a tiger anticipating a chase. "No woman makes a monkey out of me."

"I'm glad to hear it. Champagne and chivalry—that's a heady combination."

"I said I was at the reception. I didn't say I was drinking the stuff. Dom Perignon at this hour? I've got to keep a clear head for Nick's thoroughly respectable charity auction in the ballroom later."

Water dripped from his dress shirt and the hems of his formal black trousers. "Will they let you in looking like that?" she asked.

"No. Which is why I'm off to change, right after I've done something about your leg."

"Such as?"

"Taking your weight off it, for a start."

Before Sara had time to argue he swept her off her feet—but being Sara, she argued anyway. "Put me down! I can walk!"

"Relax, for goodness sake. I'm a doctor. Well, nearly." He set off across the beach. Cradling her against his body, he moved like a man who made away with women every day of the week.

Which is why he's not going to make away with me! Sara thought. "What do you mean, you're 'nearly' a doctor? Anyone from an English swot to Strangelove can call themselves doctor. And how can a doctor afford to stay at a place like this?" she asked, before

Leo Gregoryan's intoxicating masculinity could silence her.

It was an essence no amount of seawater could dilute. "Now that would be telling," was all he said.

Leo had the perfect bedside manner. He carried Sara into the summerhouse and laid her on an upholstered lounger. While she looked at the expensive coffee-table books on display in the sun-warmed retreat, he pulled a large first-aid kit from a discreet cupboard.

"I shouldn't have snapped at you earlier, Leo. I'm allergic to men who throw their weight around, and you seemed like a prime example. Sorry."

"You're forgiven. I'll put your reaction down to shock."

"I suppose you prescribe tea, hot and strong for that?" Sara asked, although he supplied enough of those qualities himself. "If that's the case, I take it with skim milk and no sugar."

His cheeks developed some interesting contours. A drop of seawater trickled down one on a voyage of exploration. "Because you're sweet enough as it is, I suppose." He sighed.

"You've heard that line before?"

"Once or twice." Breaking the seal on a pack of antiseptic wipes, he flicked it open. "Now, I'll be as gentle as I can..."

Sara gripped the arms of the lounger. Her stomach tied itself in a knot. She couldn't stand the sight of blood—especially her own—but everyone expected her to be tough. This gorgeous stranger wasn't breaking through that veneer. She stared at the sleek blue triangle of her bikini bottoms, unable to look up at him in case he spotted her nervousness. He knelt, bending over the wound on her shin. She was glad his dark curly head obscured what he was doing. When his fingertips ranged far and wide over her skin, she cleared her throat. "It's a leg, nearly-a-doctor Gregoryan."

"Thanks, but you don't have to tell me that. I came top in anatomy." His fingers slid around her calf. The action gave Sara a vivid flashback, and she winced, but the smooth skin of Leo's palm was unlike anything she'd felt before. It was amazing, and she shivered.

"You're cold." He stood and went to where Sara had spread her towel over a rock before her swim. "This is warm from the sun. Sit forward."

Instinct and experience made Sara wary about being ordered around, but her body obeyed before she could think of an excuse. As Leo swirled the candy-striped towel around her, she relaxed into its soft folds. He wasn't sending out any of the little warning signals she'd come to know all too well. If this man knew what he was doing and wanted to take charge of the situation, she was more than happy to let him.

When he cradled her leg again, Sara could hardly keep her breathing steady. She told herself all men were trouble, but how could one with hands as gentle as this have anything in common with the man she'd left behind in England?

"This may sting," he announced.

Sara tensed, but still flinched at his first touch.

"Did that hurt?" He looked up, his beautiful dark eyes serious.

"No. The wipe was cold, that's all."

He dipped his head back to his task. Sara felt his

fingers slide around to cup her calf again. She had never been pampered like this before, and loved it. As the cool, moist tissue trailed over her skin, it drew a sigh from her lips. He looked up.

"You made a good job of this abrasion," he murmured, going back to his work.

Sara was relieved enough to manage a slow smile. "I didn't notice." Because of the way the water wrapped that smart suit around you, she added in the privacy of her head.

Her rescuer seemed to be a mind reader as well. His intense gaze moved over her thigh, up the sleek lines of her body, then rose to fix on her face with an expression that pinned her to the lounger.

Sara cleared her throat and checked her watch. "Shouldn't you be working a bit faster, if you're expected back at that champagne reception?"

"I'd rather be doing this. I like to help people. The auction thing doesn't kick off for a while yet, anyway."

"You're not looking forward to it. I can tell."

"For me, doing something like this is worthwhile. Schmoozing rich people feels like pointless hard work. It's too much like the job I'll be taking on when I get back home from this holiday."

Sara leaned forward, her elbows on her knees. "Want to swap? I'd give anything to exchange all this time-wasting for a bit of shallow public relations."

He sat back on his heels, in exasperation. "How can you call staying at a five-star hotel in a beautiful place like this 'time-wasting'?"

"Because I'm offline on medical advice. That's how!"

"Then why don't you go home?"

"Because..." She gave him a calculating look. There didn't seem any point in holding back. He'd already had his hands on her. "Because my firm has swallowed the doctor's line that I could keel over with exhaustion at any time. They won't risk being sued if I die on them, and I'm not risking my job by kicking up a fuss, so here I am." She looked out at the bay. "But I'm determined to make the most of it. I'll file a report about my stay here. The executives need to know my job is still the most important thing in my life. Who knows—they may even recommend this venue to their clients."

He wasn't impressed. "I'm sure all the talk around your early grave will be about how hard you worked. Right up until the moment you dropped dead in harness."

"Not working is being dead. I was top in income generation and client satisfaction ratings for the third year running, but instead of a promotion to the board, they awarded me a holiday here 'for my outstanding contribution to the firm's success.'" She sighed. "I've been putting it off...you know how it is with work. Nobody can do my job as well as I can, but when my doctor ordered me to rest and the board backed him up, I had to give in."

He pursed his lips in a silent whistle. "If your directors are paying for you to stay here, they must think a lot of you."

She didn't react to his compliment in the way he expected. Instead, she scrunched up her face as though in pain. "I wish I could believe you. I'm determined to get that promotion, but now I've been sent here, I'm right out of the loop." She searched his expression. "For the first few hours, I was glad of the excuse to unwind. Now, with nothing else to think about, I'm beginning to wonder. Who'd want me on their board of directors, if I admit to being stressed out?"

"Any company would rather have a live employee who takes care of herself, than a dead one who's no use at all. There's no better place for a rest cure than here, that's for sure."

Sara ground her teeth. "A few days is all I need, but I'm trapped here for weeks. The company slogan is 'Want a job done properly? Let Apis Concierge Services do it.' Well, so far as I'm concerned, if you want a job done properly, get me to do it."

Leo's expression hardened. "I understand."

Caught up in her own worries, she ignored his change in mood. "I've clawed my way up from nothing, Mr Gregoryan. Now I've got the executive suite of ACS in sight. I'm never going back to skip-diving, believe me."

Her grim determination startled him. "You prefer swimming in the management goldfish bowl?" He shook his head in disbelief.

"It doesn't matter whether I enjoy it or not, Mr Gregoryan. My hard work keeps the name of ACS in the public eye. I've helped them build a multi-million pound business. When the other employees heard about my stay here, they all wanted to earn a break like it too. Which is funny, when you think about it..." She pushed out her lower lip and thought for a minute. "It's not doing me any good. I'm going mad with boredom."

"I guessed that by the way you keep looking at your watch. And if you value your phone, I wouldn't bring it onto a sandy beach with you."

Sara felt hunted. "My PA made me leave everything else behind. Can you imagine it?"

"That sounds like heaven to me. Normally, I have to escape to the Neroli to get peace and quiet." He jerked his head toward the sea.

Sara had been wondering about the beautiful yacht moored out in the bay, and gasped. "She's yours?"

He nodded. "She's big enough to get me away from it all, but the only one of my fleet that's small enough to go after mackerel shoals. Which she does very well," he added with relish.

Sara groaned. "Not another fisherman!"

"That was heartfelt!" He glanced at her hands. "You've brought your husband here for the sport fishing, have you?"

"No. There is no husband. Or partner, or boyfriend." She tapped the plain gold band on the third finger of her left hand. "I've done my time, thanks. I wear this wedding ring for protection purposes."

"So you're divorced?" He sounded as if he was stowing that fact away for future use.

Sara felt herself coloring up again. "No. We never got as far as marriage. Not that it's any of your business."

"Sorry. Put it down to my medical training. I spent years learning how to winkle out painful truths and embarrassing secrets. It's a tough habit to kick." He brushed damp curls from his forehead. "You can call me Leo, by the way."

Sara put her elbows on the arms of the lounger and leaned forward. It was good to have an excuse to study his face. "How can you afford to stay at a place like this, not-quite-a-doctor Leo? Have you majored in alternative medicine for wealthy celebrities? Or maybe you've taken out a patent on some vital pharmaceutical?"

He stared at her. Sara felt intimidated, but she hadn't clawed her way through the business jungle by blushing and backing down. She returned his stare, with interest.

"Neither," he said after the longest of pauses. "I gave up my career to take over the running of my...family firm."

"Which you must have done to stunning effect. I notice you've been very careful not to tell me what you actually do, Leo." She shot him a winning smile.

He straightened up, shutting out the sun. "I don't like talking about it. It's an unhappy story."

That put Sara's own problems into perspective. "Oh, no. I'm sorry," she said, expecting him to change the subject. Instead, he switched his attention to some distant point on the horizon, way beyond his beautiful Neroli.

"I wasn't about to throw away the dedication and work of five generations of my family. So here I am."

Sara was still curious, but his face was unreadable. She tried to provoke a reaction. "So here you are. Nearly a doctor, but actually a martyr."

His eyes flashed a warning, and he stood. Stripping off his surgical gloves gave him an excuse not to look at her. "I don't waste time thinking like that. There's no point living in the past."

"That's my motto as well." So why couldn't she put mistakes behind her? Sara watched him zip the first-aid kit and put it away. When he turned back from the cupboard, she pretended she had been studying her leg all the time. "You're the sort of tidy, methodical person who would succeed at anything, Leo. You've made a good job of my leg."

"You're not squeamish, then?"

She smiled to herself as he inspected his handiwork again. If only he knew!

"Your wound looks fine now. Leave it open to the fresh air, and it'll granulate faster than if it's covered. Put on a waterproof dressing if you go into the sea again today."

"I think I'll stick to dry land this afternoon." Sara used the towel he had put around her shoulders to blot her hair.

"Good idea. "

"I might check out the charity auction, although it's funny my PA didn't tell me anything about it." Sara frowned. "It's odd, because she knows I always want to give something back when I can."

"You can make a one-off donation of money if you like, but it's mainly an auction of promises. I suspect that's why your PA kept it quiet. You seem like a woman who'd use any excuse to work."

"I don't need an excuse. My mother was as fit as a flea until she lost her job. After that shock, she was dead within six weeks. That's not happening to me."

"Families have a lot to answer for." Leo's voice was a low growl of agreement. "My own father messed up the lives of all his children, but now I'm in charge; things are going to change. Starting right now."

Chapter Two

Leo pulled at the front of his shirt. It was already drying in the heat. "That's why I take an interest in charity events. It's the least I can do."

Sara sighed. "I know how you feel."

"Do you?" He mocked. "I very much doubt that."

She heard the echo of painful memories in his voice, but still needed to put him right. "I had to rely on the charity of other people a lot when I was younger. That's made me a keen giver."

He didn't say anything. That disappointed her. She'd been hoping he would open up, but he stayed tight-lipped. She explored another way of winning him around, and gave him a wicked look. "So what little treat are you offering to whoever wins your promise, Leo?"

"A week's expedition through the Sierra de Cadiz, based around my stud farm in Andalusia."

Sara was impressed, but puzzled. "That's incredible—but you don't sound Spanish."

"No. I come from...the eastern seaboard of Europe, but I have investments in property around the world."

Sara wondered about the micro-pause before he turned vague about his nationality. "I'm impressed. You've gone up in my estimation."

His expression hardened, and Sara recognized the look in his eyes. It stared back at her often enough from mirrors. Leo Gregoryan wasn't quick to trust. She hid a smile, wishing she'd shown a bit more of Leo's caution when she first took up with Jason, her ex. That love-rat had turned out to be far more interested in the boost Sara could give to his career than he was in her as a thinking, feeling being. "A man who likes animals can't be all bad," she added.

"You shouldn't make rash judgments." A disapproving look crossed his face.

Sara laughed out loud. "If I could ride, I'd bid for a prize like yours, Leo. Are lessons included?"

"It could be arranged. If your bid wins my promise, you're the boss."

"I'll hold you to that, although after this holiday it may be a while before I take another break from work." She blew her fringe out of her eyes, already dreading what chaos she would find when she got back to the office. "With promotion on the way, my diary will be pretty well booked up. Is there a time limit on your offer?"

"If you can't take advantage of it yourself, you could always pass the expedition on as a prize. In the same way that performance award of yours brought you here."

The chance of seeing gorgeous Leo Gregoryan riding a horse through his own land was irresistible, but Sara knew an expedition in mountains would pose problems. "That depends. How is the mobile reception in your sierra? Would I be able to get online to check my mail?"

Leo raised the perfect dark arches of his brows. "Will you want to do that in mid—expedition?"

"If I don't log in every hour, my mail builds up.

That's why I can't see the point of holidays." She didn't bother hiding her exasperation. "Instead of working a steady sixty hours a week, every week, I'm expected to hang around here, doing nothing. When they let me go back to the office, I'll have to sleep there until I've caught up with the backlog."

He exhaled in a rush. "I thought you were under orders to relax."

"I agreed because I had to." Sara dismissed his words with a casual wave of her hand. It was a lie. Inside, she felt sick. She'd had two narrow escapes in as many months. Cats were supposed to have nine lives, but people weren't so lucky. Sara knew she might not walk away the next time. She wasn't about to reveal her fears to a stranger, so she pulled a face. "Assuming that guy was a proper doctor...he had letters after his name, so I thought I'd better believe him."

"That doesn't necessarily make him a doctor!" Leo said with a derision that made her feel uncomfortable.

"Mr. Wickram has diplomas on his wall too."

"Who doesn't?" Leo drawled.

"So you do, even though you never qualified as a doctor?"

"Yes. I'm missing the only one that really matters, although qualifying would have been a mere formality."

Sara saw his straight face as another challenge. "Oh, really? I can see you've already got the 'Very Modest And I Don't Think' award!" She chuckled.

Unfazed, he grinned back. "Of course. That's a perpetual trophy. It stands right in the middle of my collection."

"If you're that much of a genius, Leo, why don't you pay someone else to run your family business while you go back and finish your medical training?"

His expression zipped up as tight as the lid of the first-aid box. "Because other people are involved."

Sara wanted to know more, but a flicker of movement pulled her attention out through the summerhouse window. A vision in black was clip-clopping down the shallow steps leading from the clifftop hotel to the sandy cove. Her business-smart pantsuit and stilettos were as out of place on the beach as Leo's outfit. Clutching an impressive organizer in one hand, she waved her arms like a tightrope walker to keep her balance on the rough concrete.

The woman called in an unrecognizable language, but she clearly wasn't happy. Her tone set Sara's teeth on edge. Someone was in big trouble.

"It's Krisia," Leo said, before speaking to the newcomer in her own language. "She's one of my entourage," he added in English, looking less than pleased.

The girl picked her way over the sand toward them. As soon as Krisia got close enough to stop concentrating on her footwork, she looked at Leo with a glittering smile. He spoke a few sharp words to her that Sara couldn't understand. Krisia shook back her mane of honey-blonde hair, and shot Sara a venomous look as Leo switched back to speaking English. "Krisia, this is Sara Astley."

"Pleased to meet you, Krisia." Sara put out her hand, but instead of taking it, the newcomer leaned into Leo and pulled at his damp clothing in a clear sign of possession. Sara felt an unexpected pang.

"I was looking for Leo," Krisia's voice shared Leo's accent, but added a dismissive sneer for Sara.

"Now you've found him, what are you going to do with him?" As if I couldn't guess, Sara thought, as Krisia clucked over her hero's wet clothes.

Ignoring Sara, Krisia spoke straight to Leo. "Everyone saw you dive into the sea and then disappear in here with this...woman, so I came to investigate."

His response was terse. "I was carrying out some first aid."

Sara smiled. It was obvious how much Leo Gregoryan hated being caught out by a woman—especially when he had his hands full with another one. At least he handled his anger much better than most men. It was her peace of mind in danger here, not her body. This stranger was a temptation her heart couldn't afford right now. She decided Krisia would have to be her unlikely ally. "It's lucky you arrived when you did, Krisia, or Leo might have been *very* late for his lunch date," she said, innocently.

It worked. Krisia glanced at Sara's fake wedding ring. Her smile turned into a possessive scowl. "You don't want to tangle with this man, Mrs. Astley."

To make sure Sara got the message, Krisia gave Leo's arm a squeeze. With the other hand, she went to poke him playfully in the stomach.

He caught her finger. Krisia snapped at him, but Sara refused to be intimidated by the little scene. "And I can guess why," she said.

Of all the times for Krisia to turn up, Leo thought. It was one of the disadvantages of having a personal shadow. She wasn't a bad girl, just a bit too keen. Pinning on a smile, he slung one arm around his cousin's shoulder. Then he drew her away from Sara, and back toward the steps leading up to the hotel. "Remind me to blunder in on you and your next hot date, Krisia."

"You know very well I don't have a boyfriend, your Majesty. All my time is spent working for you."

Leo's heart sank. Why was nothing simple any more? "Give it a rest, Krisia. I know how busy you are preparing for the coronation. I let you tag along on this break because you promised not to bother me with it. I'm putting all that ceremonial stuff to the back of my mind while I still can. Sara Astley was helping me."

"Like all the others."

"No." Leo was sure about that. "She doesn't recognize me. Not even when you pranced up waving the royal crest for everyone to see."

Krisia snorted, turning the leather-bound organizer around to hide the blue, gold, and red crest of Kharova. "She's softening you up, like every gold digger before her."

"If it's a line, it's a new one. And I like it." He grinned. "I thought you were playing tennis this morning. You're supposed to be taking it easy too."

"How can I? I'm too busy with your arrangements!"

They reached the bottom of the steps leading to the hotel. Krisia moved in closer, but Leo peeled himself from her grasp. He was good at letting people down gently, but none of his methods worked on Krisia. Boundaries were difficult where she was concerned. As a close relative of Kharova's royal family, Krisia had always been around. That hadn't been a problem while Leo's older brother was alive. Zacari had been destined to rule, while the younger Gregoryans were all equals.

Now Zac was dead. Leo had been landed with the top job, and Krisia was finding it hard to adjust to his new position in life.

"Don't remind me. I'm trying to forget. And it's why I don't want you to give the game away. I'm here to enjoy myself. That's all. Nick's agreed not to blow my cover. You must promise to do the same. You do not tell this woman who I am."

"Yes, your Majesty." Her expression was sulky. "Of course. I came to tell you a change of clothes is ready in your suite. You'll need them after tangling with that Astley woman."

"Her name is Sara." There was a warning in his voice, but it was a gentle one.

Krisia huffed. "I don't know how you remember them all."

"And I don't know why you can't forget any of them!" Leo glanced back toward the summerhouse, weighing the brief pleasure of inviting Sara to lunch against the prospect of Krisia moaning about his other conquests for the rest of the day. Then he checked his watch and cursed. "I'll be up to shower and change as soon as I can."

Krisia's scrutiny was like sandpaper. "I suppose that means you're going back to her."

Leo wriggled his shoulders, trying to unstick his drying shirt from his body. "I'm going to give Sara some practical help. She had a slight accident. While I enjoy the chance to deal with it, you can tell Nick he'll need to restock the first-aid kit in the summerhouse."

Krisia scowled. "You enjoy yourself too often, Leo."

He tousled her hair. "It's allowed. I'm not twenty-eight yet. That isn't old—and don't you forget it!"

"Don't worry, I won't."

"Good. Carry on then. I've got to get back to the summerhouse, but once I've finished down there, I'll be up to get ready for lunch. Ten minutes, tops."

"Make sure you are," Krisia said.

Leo had never been late for anything in his life, but he didn't correct her. All he did was smile. He knew how much Krisia needed to be wanted. If working for him made her happy, then he wouldn't disappoint her without good reason.

Sara blinked in pretended surprise as Leo forged his way back into the summerhouse.

"Sorry about that, Sara. I'm having lunch with Nick, so I'll have to get a move on. I'll carry you up to the hotel, then it's good-bye for a while. Duty calls."

She rearranged the towel around her shoulders, trying to look as prim as a Greek matron. It didn't work. "Don't let me distract you, Leo. If you want to head off, be my guest. I can manage, and I'm the last person to get between anyone and their public image."

He muttered something under his breath. "You and I are both here to get away from all that." The cynicism showed in her face. Leo pretended to ignore it, and carried on. "Krisia's an assistant of mine."

"A very personal assistant, from the way she's keeping watch on you."

"She's a member of my staff. That's all."

"I'll bet." Sara noticed he was watching her hands. Looking down she realized she was fiddling with her ring, thumbing it round on her finger. She stopped.

"Somebody's given you a very jaundiced opinion of men, Sara, but we aren't all the same."

"Oh, no? The way you talk about Krisia makes you sound pretty glib."

Leo held up his hands. "Okay. You've got me there. Guilty as charged. There are plenty of women willing to be in my life, but there's no need for me to tangle with Krisia. Besides, it would be too close to home."

"But you admit you do fool around with women, whenever you get the chance?" Sara asked, wondering how he'd try to wriggle out of it.

"Yes. What's wrong with that?"

"People get hurt."

"Not the way I do it."

His arrogance almost took her breath away. "You are so sure of yourself, aren't you?"

He lifted one shoulder in a shrug. "No. Simply careful."

"About what?"

"About the type of woman I 'fool around with,' as you so delicately put it. They say if you stroke a seal pup, it'll follow you everywhere. Well, cute and cuddly, I'm okay with. Big, soulful eyes are a plus, but I can do without the constant adoration, thanks very much. I'm not that much of a control freak. I like my encounters brief and uncomplicated."

"So you admit it. You are completely feckless!"

He laughed. "If the mood takes me, I can throw off convention and have a good time. I've never had any complaints. When it comes to women, I'm interested in passing pleasures. Not permanent arrangements."

His gaze locked on to Sara, alert to the smallest changes in her expression. She could feel it, and wondered if he could tell she had no intention of getting involved with anyone again either. Gazing into his darkly seductive eyes, she tried to remember how good a simple fling could be. Once, there had been no room in her life for anything but work and the occasional night out with the girls. Then she took up with Jason. He turned out to be a real cuckoo in the nest, subtly undermining all her other friendships. Before she knew it, he'd taken over her life. Sara became not much more than his hotline to the decision makers at ACS. Instead of him being her 'plus one' at parties, he did all the talking, expecting her to hang on his words as well as his arm.

The less valued Sara felt, the harder she'd worked to become the best at her job. Apis Concierge Solutions became an outlet for all her energy. Her escape route eventually gave her the confidence to rebel, and throw Jason out. Now she was alone again. Hard work had made her a success, but she had no one left to share it with.

Her memories stung more than the wound on her shin. Making a superhuman effort not to wince, Sara levered herself up from the sun-lounger and took a few steps. "If you've been invited to lunch, I must let you go. Thanks for sorting me out. My leg feels much better."

"Of course it does. I have healing hands."

Sara rolled her eyes. "Your arrogance is something else!" She was teasing, because this time he couldn't be challenged. He had a smile that took all the pain away, reminding her how good life could be. "But on this occasion, I'll admit you're right, Leo."

"You shouldn't pass up the chance of a little more pampering. As your qualified first aider, I couldn't possibly make you walk all the way up to the hotel," he said with another dose of winning charm.

This time Sara didn't argue when he slipped one arm beneath her shoulders and lifted her. "I should warn you, Leo, I've got no head for heights."

"Don't worry. Leave everything to me. All you have to do is hang on tight."

She was beautifully built, and perfectly balanced. Leo carried her up the flight of steps, and then whisked her straight to her suite.

"My key card's threaded onto my bikini top and tucked down inside so I don't lose it in the water," she said as he set her down on her feet outside the door. Raising her hands, she untied the plaited strings around her neck and fumbled around inside her top. Leo felt a powerful surge of interest. He checked his watch. Women were never slow in coming on to him, but this must be some kind of record.

"That looks like fun." He covered her hands with his own. "What can I do? Hold up your straps while you do that, or fish around in there for you?" The reverberation of his voice low in his throat made him feel mischievous.

It seemed to have the opposite effect on her. She clamped her hands to her chest, shutting him out. At first he thought she was playing hard to get, but when he laughed she took a small step away from him. The look on her face made him uncomfortably aware that flirting in the sunshine was one thing. Once a woman and a man were alone together with no witnesses, they both had to be careful.

The situation was getting serious.

"Neither. I can manage, thanks," she snapped.

Holding one strap between her teeth, she freed the rectangle of plastic then retied her top with a firm knot at the nape of her neck.

"Pity. Game fishing's one of my hobbies." Leo gave her a smile guaranteed to defuse any situation. Except this one, he discovered.

"I'm sure it is—but I can guess what you were hoping to catch on that expedition."

"More than the cold shoulder I got, that's for sure."

She tensed, but Leo didn't see why he should move away. He'd done nothing wrong, and he was enjoying the view. Although Sara was as slender and toned as an athlete, she had curves in all the right places, and as her hair dried it came alive with rich copper tones.

"I'm sure you'll understand if I don't invite you into my suite, Leo."

"No, but I'm a forgiving kind of a guy. I won't hold it against you. Unless you ask me to, that is."

The tension broke like meringue, and she smiled. "You wish! You're an out-and-out rogue. I can see that from here."

"At least I'm honest about it, Sara. And now, if you'll excuse me, Nick's expecting me down on the terrace," he added.

"Go on, then. I don't want to get the blame for making you late. You still have to get ready, don't forget." She turned her back on him and limped into her suite.

He waited until she deadlocked the door. Then he strolled off to his own suite to allow himself the luxury of thinking about Sara Astley under a power shower.

Chapter Three

Sara ate lunch on the balcony of her suite wondering what to do with the rest of the day. That was a problem she never faced at home. Work filled all the gaps in her life. Here, the sun shone through them so brightly there was no escape.

The tempting treats prepared by a team of brilliant chefs were nothing like the tasteless sandwiches she ate al desko at home. Food here was designed to be savored, not scoffed. For Sara, the everyday urge to bolt it down and get onto the next task was irresistible. She soon regretted it. Separated from her inbox, there was nothing to hurry for. All she could do now was sit and wait for the next meal.

Below, the sea was as restless as she felt. The memory of Leo Gregoryan carrying her back from the beach kept doing funny things to her. She wriggled her toes, remembering the feel of his arms around her body. Her lapis-painted toenails twinkled in the relentless sunshine. Meeting Leo had cheered her up, and whetted her appetite. She wanted to see him again, but she was wary. The last thing she needed was a man in her life.

She fiddled with the silver cutlery on the lunch tray, sending sunbeams dancing. It was hard to admire the bone china plates and fine crystal glasses laid out in front of her when she was busy worrying about what might be going on back in the offices of ACS.

She hated taking time off. It let her mind freewheel. That was never a good thing. She was scared her chances of promotion were wrecked, but her body had been running on adrenaline for too long. Her PA, Jo, had booked everything. That meant she knew all Sara's secrets—or at least, most of them. The hotel had been instructed that on no account were they to let Sara hire a car during her stay.

At the time, Sara's nerves had been in such a state, she'd agreed. Now she felt trapped inside the spa complex. At work, she spent all her time doing everything for her clients. Here, other people were in charge, and it felt weird. Everything from food to entertainment was available instantly. All she had to do was pick up the phone and call room service. It was supposed to be relaxing, but it felt unnatural.

She studied the last few streaks of chocolate parfait on the dessert plate as though it were a work of art. Lunch had been the closest thing to heaven since she'd been carried up from the beach in the arms of that hunk Leo Gregoryan, but it would be a long time before dinner arrived.

She sighed, wishing she could have holidayed at home. That had never been an option. In her heart, she knew her PA was right to make her leave the country. It took away the temptation of dropping into the office, to check up on things. The trouble was, with her appointments diary more than fifteen hundred miles away Sara was missing it like a lover.

Work is more satisfying than any man, she reminded herself...although rogue male Leo Gregoryan was an interesting distraction.

There's no harm in a bit of harmless window

shopping, is there? Not even when I'm looking at a man like him!

From her suite, there were breathtaking views in every direction over the formal terraced gardens of the hotel. In contrast, the window in her office back at home looked straight out at a brick wall. That suited Sara. With no distractions, she could work harder and longer than anyone else. She got all the rest and recreation she needed from visiting clients, and supervising the stunning garden parties and receptions she organized for them.

At least, that was what she told herself until she arrived at this magnificent hotel, and experienced the beautiful suite. The stylish glass and chrome was cool in the heat of the day, and its stunning, silent simplicity was balm to her soul.

She got up and wandered through to the bedroom, with its sweet-pea color scheme and massive circular bed. She felt like a visitor to another world, and wished her mom were alive to share in all this luxury.

Picking up the latest copy of *Vogue* from the coffee table in the lounge, she flicked through it. For five years she had been arranging this kind of luxury for her ACS clients. At last, she was living the dream herself. Outside, the cornflower-blue of the sky was absorbed by the sea and deepened to opulent ultramarine. A light breeze lifted the gauzy muslin curtains fluttering beside the French doors leading to her balcony. She thought back to the ACS offices in London. State-of-the-art air-conditioning meant none of their windows opened.

Moving back out onto the balcony, she pulled in a big breath. It was full of the sweet, spicy fragrance of summer. At the Paradise Hotel, the usual herb-scented dust of the countryside was overlaid with floral tones of the surrounding gardens and their well-watered lawns. You couldn't take great lungfuls of fresh air like this in the city. Closing her eyes, she tipped back her head and felt bright warmth flowing straight from the sun right into her body and soul.

An unusual noise out in the garden shattered her peace and quiet. Annoyed, she opened her eyes and scowled down at the disturbance. A man in tennis whites had knocked into one of the sun loungers in his hurry to pick up a book.

"Clumsy idiot," she said. It came out louder than she intended, and he looked up just as the frantic voice of Leo's PA rose in panic. Alarmed, the man missed his grip on the book. It slipped out of his hands, bounced off the edge of the lounger and disappeared between two large planters of heliotropes.

"I thought I heard...Ah!" Leo felt a rush of relief when he spotted Sara, although a pretty girl was more likely to add to his troubles than save his skin. "She'll have a good view of the garden from there, Krisia." Swallowing his doubts he waved at Sara as she leaned on the rail of her balcony. For a split second, the thought of their last meeting danced through his mind. Then the clouds closed in on him again. "We're looking for Krisia's organizer. She thinks she left it on the terrace, after the reception. Can you see it?'

"There was a guy looking at something like it down here." She pointed to the lounger. Leo looked, but couldn't see anyone. More importantly, he couldn't see the book either. The terrace was deserted.

"Oh...he's gone." Sara sounded disappointed.

Disappointment was nothing compared to what

Leo would feel if that book fell into the wrong hands. The arrangements for his coronation were complete. Now it turned out that against his wishes, Krisia was keeping a written copy of the timetable and most of the important contact details in her organizer.

"What guy? Where?" He tried to keep the anger out of his voice, but Krisia was already on the move. She'd seen something. Darting forward, she retrieved the lost book from between the two planters of purple flowers.

Leo let out his breath in a long stream of relief. His mind had been a maelstrom from the moment Krisia told him her organizer was missing. He felt like giving her a real rollocking, but there was no point in losing his temper now. The crisis was over. "No harm done, this time. But you were lucky."

"I know," she said, with genuine anguish.

"Then we'll let that be your punishment." Leo told her.

Someone else wasn't so forgiving. "Been letting your work get on top of you, Krisia? I always keep my mind on business," Sara called, although her raised eyebrow was aimed at Leo.

I'll bet you do, Leo thought. So did I, until you swam into my life.

Krisia scowled at her, but Leo had the perfect answer ready. "That's why they sent you here, Sara." He grinned.

Sara had to admit he had a point. Perhaps ACS was right, and she did need a holiday. Watching Leo and his PA walk away, she came to a grudging conclusion. The temptations of work paled in comparison to this place. Like a dormouse coming out of hibernation, Sara decided to find out what she'd been missing in the outside world. The charity auction would be a good place to start.

Selecting a pink sundress, she pushed bare feet into a pair of white sandals.

If the auction's too slow, I can go outside and work on my tan. She headed toward the door. Her brand-new pedometer lay on the table.

Shimmying her dress up, she clipped the device onto her lacy briefs then checked her appearance in a full-length mirror. The step-counter's slimline shape hardly showed. That made her smile. Her doctor's instructions were to make time for exercise, and Leo had told her to take more care of herself. This secret gesture was a hat-tip to them both. She'd start clocking up the miles by taking the stairs instead of the lift.

A murmur of conversation rose to greet her as she walked along the upper hallway above the Paradise Hotel's lobby. The double doors to one of the reception rooms on the ground floor stood open in the heat. People straggled in from the sunshine, heading toward the bar at the far end of the huge room. As she looked around for more details of the auction of promises, a tall figure detached itself from the throng and started toward her.

It was Leo.

He looked perfect in a fresh tuxedo and crisp white shirt. Sara's heart gave a lurch. As he worked his way through the crowd, she composed her opening shot. "You've dried off well, Mr. Gregoryan."

He grinned. "My hand-picked team always has a spare set of everything to hand."

Sara put her head on one side and regarded him.

"Including women?"

He pushed one hand into his pocket. Jingling his change, he rocked back on his highly polished shoes. "What can I say? With so many delightful examples around, it would be a sin to ration myself."

"As the bishop said to the actress."

"You already know I'm no bishop." His voice was low and provocative. Sara's smile faded. "What's the matter, Sara? Don't tell me you've been struck dumb by my honesty."

"I was waiting for you to say 'and you're not an actress.' Don't say it didn't occur to you."

He laughed. But he didn't say yes—and he didn't say no, either.

"Thanks for your help earlier, Sara."

"It was nothing. But you want to watch that PA of yours. She took her eye off the ball," she said, her heart sinking as Krisia pushed her way through the crowd toward them. "This is the second time she's arrived as if by magic."

"She's been checking out the lot number for my promise. You must excuse me while I go and discuss the details with her." He put his hand on Sara's arm, and squeezed gently.

Sara smiled before she remembered this was the same softening-up process all men used on unsuspecting women. "Don't worry about me. I've got to check if they'll register a late promise from me."

Leo raised his dark arched eyebrows. "What are you doing?"

Sara gave him a smile that promised more than her lips offered. "As I've got nothing to do here but think, I had a flash of inspiration. I'm not supposed to do any

ACS work, but nobody can object to me offering my services for charity, can they? So, I'm promising an hour's lifestyle consultation to anyone who can relieve the tedium of my holiday by offering the highest bid."

Leo made a dismissive noise. "I'd say every guest here has all the lifestyle they can handle, and more."

Sara wouldn't let him put her off. "That's not the point. It's raising money for a good cause. Besides, everybody needs a troubleshooter in their life once in a while."

"Troubleshooter?"

"The firm I work for solves problems people don't even know they have. Party planning, executive travel, project management, personal assistance of every kind from translations to accompanying child travelers around the world, squeezing twenty-five hours out of every day—name your problem and we'll solve it."

Leo was about to say something, but then his PA reached his side. Angling her body to shut Sara out, Krisia spoke to Leo in his own language and pointed toward a large woman draped in gold jewelry, who stood beside the bar. The lady twinkled her fingers at Leo.

"Excuse me, Sara. Krisia says Mrs. Revere wants to discuss the offer I've put up for auction. I'll catch you later."

He surged off through the crowd, leaving Sara to stare at his broad, beautifully tailored back. As he worked his way through the room, she wondered whether she would ever see him again. He was the sort of guy who couldn't move without other people exchanging a few words or a smile in passing.

Once she had registered her own promise, Sara

took a seat on one of the velvet-covered chairs before a low dais at the front of the room. She soon discovered this charity auction was in a different league from the ones she'd attended back at home. She'd been looking forward to bidding for Leo's expedition, but her spirits took a dive as she studied the electronic display on a screen above the auctioneer's rostrum. The reserve prices alone were ten times the value of her offering. There was the lease of an ocean-going yacht, a six-month-old helicopter to be re-sprayed in the purchaser's choice of colors, and dozens of cases of vintage wines. Each could be expected to raise a small fortune in bids. This audience didn't deal in fiddling small change. Sara would have felt good handing a sizable sum over to charity to win Leo's luxury break, but the auctioneer started the bidding way beyond the absolute maximum she could have afforded. In the end, the place on his weekend expedition went to Mrs. Revere for half a million dollars. Sara gulped. That woman had serious money, as well as good taste.

Making a mental note to give Mrs. Revere her business card, Sara turned in her seat to look for the woman. The first person she spotted was Leo. He sat on the far side of the room, flanked by Krisia and a chunky man in a smart suit and sinister dark glasses. Several members of the audience had security men in tow, so that didn't surprise Sara as much as what Leo did next. When details of the consultation she was offering were read out, he nodded at the auctioneer to open the bidding. Straight away, other people joined in.

Leo drove up the offers at lightning speed. Sara watched open-mouthed as he inspired the audience to try to outbid him. Soon the competition was between

Leo and Mrs. Revere. In the end, Leo increased his bid to one hundred fifty thousand dollars for an hour of Sara's time. At that, Mrs. Revere laughed and shook her head. The auctioneer's gavel dropped with a bang, and the crowd erupted in applause.

The thought of spending an hour in private consultation with Leo Gregoryan sent Sara's internal thermostat off the scale. Alone with him for sixty minutes, it would take all her willpower to ignore his flashing dark eyes, and that generous, sensual mouth.

A man who was so good-looking had to be trouble. A ripple of movement ran through the other side of the audience, and she saw Leo moving along his row of seats toward the central aisle. He was heading in her direction. From that moment, the auction lost its appeal for her. All she could think about was what might happen next, and how she could cope. Desperate to explain herself, she jumped up and stumbled past the other people in her row. "Leo! Can I speak to you for a minute?"

"I was about to ask you the same thing." He summoned a waiter. "What would you like to drink, Sara?"

"A mineral water over ice with a twist, please."

"That's a good choice in this heat." He ordered a jug of Glacier and two glasses. "You're an unusual woman. I thought you'd want to toast my winning bid in vintage champagne."

"I'd rather give the extra money to charity instead. That's what I wanted to talk to you about. You know you've paid way over the odds for an hour of my time, don't you?"

"That's what all this is about. Money is the least of

my worries. Besides, I'm sure you'll give me excellent value"—his smile gave a hint of hidden meaning to his words—"so I was going to stop at nothing to win your promise."

Her body surged with sudden, unfamiliar need.

"This way I can keep you under observation. And make sure you don't work too hard." His words were supposed to be comforting. They had the opposite effect on Sara.

He guided her outside, and into the shade of an arbor draped with fragrant jasmine. Playing doctors and nurses with Leo would be interesting, she thought as the waiter poured her a glass of water, but *I'm not going to risk asking for details.*

"I'm sorry you missed out to Mrs. Revere for my lot." He clicked his tongue. "She made a great offer, but I can't see her sleeping under the stars, or learning to make a fire without matches."

"Now you're teasing! There's never any danger of a lady like that getting her hands dirty. Your prize will soon be doing the rounds of the New England charity auctions." Sara chuckled.

"That's a shame. It would have been fun to have Mrs. Revere travel to Spain and enter into the spirit of the thing."

Sara gazed at him, amazed anyone would think a woman like that would be interested in fresh air. "Mrs. Revere is no more likely to go on your expedition in the Spanish mountains than you are to lead it, Leo."

He flexed his body. "I've done it plenty of times in the past." His shoulders dropped. "It'll be good to do it one last time."

The thought of Leo astride a plunging Andalusian

stallion was a big distraction. She tried to push it to the back of her mind. "My guess is it'll be a long time before anyone cashes in your offer. I've been to charity auctions where the same bottle of sixty-year-old Scotch had been doing the rounds for months."

A strange look came over Leo's face. "Were you serious about taking that trip of mine?"

"Sort of. I hadn't really thought it through. I wouldn't have any more idea of how to light a fire than Mrs. Revere."

"Maybe not, but anyone can enjoy a trip like that. Why don't I take you on a mini-expedition? It will help you forget your work."

Sara took a long drink of mineral water to hide her disbelief. "It must be thousands of miles from here to Andalusia. And I've told you—I can't ride."

Leo waved aside her concerns with a lazy gesture. "I have a friend who owns an estate on the mainland here. We'll sail over on the Neroli and borrow a couple of horses from him. It won't take my people long to check everything out and arrange the catering."

"Catering?" Sara twisted her fake wedding ring.

"You'd want to make a day of it?"

"Well...yes." She had serious doubts about the horse riding part of Leo's fantasy, but a day in the mountains with him would be the ideal way to make her enforced holiday fly by. She'd deal with the riding when, and if, it happened.

"Good. Then we'll go tomorrow. I'll get someone on it straight away. What time would you like to leave here?"

Sara fizzed with nervous anticipation, but she was careful to speak as if she was arranging a site meeting with a client. "How about eight a.m.?"

"Fine. We can breakfast on the Neroli."

Sara tried not to think what it would be like to eat anything on board a boat that wasn't as big and stable as a cruise liner.

Leo signaled to his bulky security man, who was now roaming the perimeter of the room. After giving him a few murmured instructions, he turned back to Sara with a smile. "It's all fixed. My escape into the mountains and your first riding lesson all arranged, as requested."

"That was impressive."

He looked puzzled. "What?"

"You've sorted out the trip of a lifetime for me in minutes, and there's going to be catering too!"

"All it takes is a dedicated team."

"I know. It's just that I'm usually the one running the show."

"Then it'll be a great way for you to experience life on the other side of the velvet rope, for once." In a smooth movement he lifted her hand to his lips and kissed it. "Until we meet again. Tomorrow, at eight a.m., sharp." His smile told Sara she might have a lot more to worry about in the morning than seasickness and horses.

A few hours later, Leo was picking out tunes on a grand piano in the café bar of the Paradise Hotel.

"Our country spent too many years speculating who your late brother would marry. You shouldn't encourage the media by having a holiday romance, Your Majesty," his bodyguard said, lounging against the instrument.

"I have no idea what you're talking about. Any

woman who is as obsessed with her career as Sara Astley has her hands far too full to juggle a crown as well. And stop calling me 'Your Majesty.' You know the rules while we're here. I'm Leo Gregoryan. That's all."

"You don't want to have anything to do with that woman, Leo. I've checked her out online. She works for a firm boasting they'll 'arrange anything legal' for its clients. That sounds a very risky prospect to me." Krisia's mouth was a tight line of disapproval.

Leo slammed his hands onto the piano keys with a discordant crash. He looked at his PA in disgust. "I'm supposed to be getting away from everything, Krisia. Why bring it all back to me?"

"There's less than a month until your coronation," she hissed. "I've got the best interests of our country, and you, at heart."

"Then stop reminding me how fast my time as a free man is disappearing. I'm amazed you haven't installed an electronic countdown clock ready for the off, like they put in Trafalgar Square before the London Olympics.'

"It's funny you should say that, Your Majesty. One of those went up in the public square outside the palace yesterday," the security man said.

Leo groaned. "Then that's another reason not to hurry home. How many more times do I have to remind you? I'm here incognito."

"We are yours to command, Your Maj—I mean...sir." Krisia blushed.

Leo's attention had been grabbed by a woman walking into the room, so he never noticed his PA's slip. While waiters fussed around the newcomer, Leo took the opportunity to study her. It took several seconds to realize it was Sara. Tonight, the toned legs he remembered so well were hidden beneath a long, shimmering evening dress. He'd been intending to get Krisia to confirm with Sara the arrangements for their trip to the mainland the next day. Seeing his quarry sashay across the room, her rich auburn hair flowing loose around her shoulders, he had a better idea. Once Sara finished dinner, he would stroll over and ask her himself.

Leo wasn't the only one watching Sara's every move. "She's a looker, but she's got quite a prison pallor," Leo's bodyguard said.

"That's probably something to do with the amount of Factor 50 she got all over His Majesty's clothes this morning," Krisia said.

Leo gave a deep, throaty chuckle. "That didn't worry me. And this glorious Greek sun will soon toast her like an almond." He said, "Long Journey" whispering from his fingers to accompany Sara all the way to her table in the restaurant.

Sara had planned to eat in her room, but whenever she was alone, there could be no hiding from the truth. The company of other people stopped her thinking too hard about all the mistakes she'd made. A staggering view of the Aegean, chilled orange juice on tap, and full air-conditioning didn't make up for the buzz of conversation she could find in the restaurant.

She was dimly aware of a piano playing in the bar area as she entered. After she was seated, she had time to look around. The waiter fussed over lighting the display of candles in the centre of her table, but Sara's eyes were drawn toward the Steinway. With a jolt, she recognized the player.

It was Leo Gregoryan.

He sat in shirtsleeves, his jacket and tie draped over the chair beside him. The contrast between his gleaming white shirt, dark halo of hair and golden skin almost took her breath away.

Sara was impressed, and so was Krisia. She leaned against the piano drooling over Leo as he idled through a slow, romantic tune. Then he glanced up from the keys. His eyes locked onto Sara's. He smiled, and her heart flipped. Before she could get it under control, he began to play a mesmerizing version of "What Makes You Beautiful." Krisia shot her a look of catlike disdain.

Dining alone didn't feel like such a good idea any more. Inviting Leo and his PA to join her was the obvious solution. It would thank him for fixing her leg that morning, and give them all a chance to get to know each other before she embarrassed herself the next day.

With that woman breathing down his neck, Sara felt Leo would be distracted, and she wouldn't be tempted by him. Taking out one of her business cards, she scribbled a note on the back. *Leo, would you and Krisia like to join me for dinner?* Ordering a Cinderella, she asked the waiter to deliver the card.

While his hands occupied themselves on the piano keys, Leo watched Sara out of the corner of his eye. When she passed something to a waiter, he went back to concentrating on his music. Probably a message to her PA, he thought, and started to dream up arousing ways of distracting Sara from her work.

The waiter beelined for the group at the piano. As he reached Leo's elbow, he held out a business card.

Krisia snatched it, read the message then pushed it at Leo with a scowl. "It's from your new conquest."

Puzzled, Leo took it from her, then exclaimed. "That's the first time a woman's ever asked me to dinner. What an opportunity!"

"You're not going to accept are you, Your—I mean, Leo?"

"Why not? It'll be fun. Much better than sitting around killing time. You can both take the rest of the evening off," he told his staff. "I'll be fine for a few hours."

His bodyguard sniffed. "Are you sure, sir? I mean, Miss Astley doesn't look to be a threat, but other people might be."

Krisia pounced on the argument. "Yes, what's the point of having a bodyguard if you don't let him do his job?"

Leo cleared his throat in a warning. "That's enough, Krisia. I've told you before. You're my PA, not my mother. I'm capable of fending off an attack with a loaded dessert spoon, which is the only danger in a place like this. Good night!"

With a face like thunder, Krisia swept off. The security man slouched along in her wake. Once his entourage had vanished, Leo wrote a quick note of his own and then summoned a waiter.

Sara saw the flurry of activity over at the piano as she sipped her drink. She tried not to notice, but couldn't help wondering if it was her note that threw the stick of dynamite into their little fishpond.

As she studied the menu, her mobile rang. Grabbing it into silence, she whispered into the mic.

"Sara?" Leo's honeyed tones sent a tingle straight

through her body. "Thanks for your offer, but I must refuse. I never accept invitations from strange women in bars. And I've told you before, Krisia is my PA, not my companion."

She looked up. On the other side of the room, he inclined his head toward her.

"Yes, but does she know that?" she replied.

There was a pause. They watched each other across the busy restaurant. Sara dodged about to keep him in sight as waiters and diners went to and fro across their sightline. Leo was motionless. "Of course."

"Are you sure?" Sara said.

"About dinner? Yes."

"That isn't what I meant—"

"Now, please go back to your room, Sara."

She couldn't believe her ears. Who was this guy, thinking he could give her orders? Men always tried it on, but he was different—or so she thought. "How dare you?" she asked, but Leo had already cut the call.

How could anyone say that? She wasn't going to miss her dinner for him. Stuffing the phone back into her bag, Sara made a big show of updating her list of contacts, then checked her makeup—anything rather than do what Leo Gregoryan told her to do.

When the waiter returned to take her order, he brought a message as well. "A bouquet has been delivered to your suite, Miss Astley."

Flowers? Sara caught her breath. No one had ever sent her flowers before. She ought to feel excited. Instead she felt sick. They must be from Jason, her ex. Sara's PA had promised not to tell him where she was. The girl must have buckled under his pressure. Sara had told Jason often enough how she wished he'd make a romantic gesture like this, but he'd never taken the hint. Why did he have to pull such a stunt now, when she was feeling so vulnerable?

"They are from the gentleman at the piano, madam," the waiter added, while Sara was still wondering how to put her horror into words. When he said that, she almost stopped breathing. She looked up. Leo was busy putting on his tie. It was a relief to know he'd sent the flowers, but it did nothing to calm her nerves. Did that make him less dangerous, or more?

"W-was there a message?"

"Oh, yes, madam. I shall fetch it for you." The waiter bowed, and left. He came back with a small card.

In my country, the man does the asking. *Would you like to join me for dinner, Miss Astley?*

Sara smiled, ready to give the waiter her reply. There was no need.

Leo Gregoryan was heading straight for her table, like a cat about to get the cream.

Chapter Four

"Have you ordered, Sara?" Leo eased out the chair beside her and sat.

"Not yet. But when I do, I'll do it myself. Please don't order for me."

He accepted a menu from the waiter. "Do you expect me to overrule you?" he asked.

"It's been known." Sara struggled to keep the bitterness out of her voice.

He closed his menu and reached for hers. "The beef here is superb, and so are the sorbets. You'll love it all. I speak from experience."

Sara had such a grip on her menu that he let it go. "I'll have the fish," she told him. "And I never touch dessert."

"But you accept flowers from strangers." His words were terse.

"They were a wonderful gesture. I'm sure they're lovely," Sara said with dignity, although she couldn't wait to find out what had been delivered to her suite.

He leaned low across the table, toward her. "That's the first of many gestures, Sara." His voice was as seductive as the candlelight.

She made a performance of closing her menu and placing it down on top of his. "Let's get a couple of things straight right now, Leo. One: You've paid for an hour of my time, so I'm assuming that's why you're here. You've got about fifty-five minutes of your time left. Two: I don't do one-night stands. So save the charm, and your money, and start talking."

He drew back with a poise she envied. "You make me glad I didn't have the florist deliver the bouquet straight to your table. You might have smacked me with it. There's something you should know, too, Sara. In my country, women trample over each other to win my favor. Those I choose enjoy the best of everything, and make no secret of their enjoyment."

"It doesn't sound as if your country goes much on women's lib."

"It is not like Docklands, that's true."

"You've obviously been checking up on me."

"In my position, it pays to be careful." His eyes were thoughtful. He didn't speak again until they had given their order to the waiter. Then he leaned forward a second time, lowering his voice to a whisper. "I've made the right choice in you. It may have been for the wrong reasons, but a man like me must be adaptable. So, let's get down to business in what remains of our time together. While I was busy with the auctioneer, my PA was looking you up online. Apis Concierge Solutions is an interesting prospect. I've been wondering about your firm's claim to take on anything legal. You say you pride yourself on your discretion. We're both busy people. You need a relaxing time, and I could do with bouncing a few ideas around. When you sent your card to me, I decided to combine a delightful dinner with the consultation I secured with you."

Sara had been in business for too long to let a client see her excitement bubble up at the prospect of an hour's work. "That suits me," she said, then jumped, her eyes wide. For the second time, the unmistakable sound of a ring tone floated from the floor under her chair. "Oh, no! What can I say, Leo—how unprofessional!" She snatched up her bag and scrabbled inside it for her phone.

"Don't apologize. I never heard a thing," Leo said, as she grimaced at the screen. "Although as your on-site medical advisor, I ought to insist you send that device straight back to your suite."

"I'll do better than that. I'll take it there myself," she muttered, sweeping off toward the lift. She was glad he hadn't suggested going with her. If he'd done that, he would have found out she'd arranged the call herself—partly to stop Leo getting above himself, but mostly for the chance to go and see the first flowers she had ever been sent.

Thirty seconds later, Sara flung open the door of her suite. She was greeted by the voluptuous scent of lilies, and the sight of a starburst of flowers arranged on the coffee table of her lounge. They were so lovely, she knew she'd never be able to look at Leo in the same way again.

Taking three long, lingering breaths of the expensive atmosphere, she tried to clear her head. He'd suggested this was his opening shot at seduction. She ought to hate him for it, but that was impossible. The flowers were such an amazing gesture.

Throwing her phone onto the settee, she marched back to the restaurant and took her place at the table.

"I'm so sorry about that, Leo. Now, as this is a business meeting, you'll want your..." She left an almost imperceptible pause before saying, "PA in attendance."

"No. In fact, I've dismissed my team for the evening."

Alarm bells rang inside Sara's head. "Why? I've already told you this is on a purely professional basis."

"I wouldn't approach you for anything less, Sara. The fact is, I'd appreciate the advice of an unbiased observer on a...delicate matter. My whole entourage is handpicked and I'm certain of their loyalty, but that's a big part of my problem. No one will risk telling me I'm wrong. At times, I need to talk hardheaded business sense. My current bunch of yes-men and women are delightful, but they aren't always useful."

"And Krisia is in love with you. That's bound to cloud her judgment."

"Rubbish," he said after a moment's pause, but she could see her words had rattled him. "Don't change the subject. The truth is, none of them talk straight to me. You do."

It sounded like praise, but Sara was on the alert for empty flattery. "Then I'll start as I mean to go on, Leo. You might as well have left your jacket and tie at the piano. There's no need to overheat on my account."

"I wouldn't say that." There was a definite double entendre in his voice. "Nick has a strict dress code for this part of the restaurant. We have a deal. He does everything to respect my privacy. I respect his rules."

"Really? The more you don't tell me about yourself, Leo Gregoryan, the more intrigued I am."

He smiled. "That's how I like it."

Not for the first time, Sara thought how sexy Leo looked in a tux. As he unbuttoned his jacket and pulled out his cuffs, she had another drink. As an attempt to distract herself, it was useless. "Then start bouncing your ideas, mystery man."

"First, I must be sure you'll treat everything I say with absolute confidentiality."

Sara nodded.

Though he said, "Fine," his body language told a different story. He linked his hands in front of him on the tablecloth. Then he sat back, gnawing his lip. Finally, he threw his arms wide. "I owe it to a lot of people, including many generations of my family, to make a success of my new job."

Sara leaned forward, expecting to find out at last what had made him abandon his career. "And this job would be...?"

He took a sip of wine. As she watched, the embers of passion began glowing deep inside her. He was good-looking, for sure, but something else about him grabbed her attention and held it, tight. "I've inherited all my father's lands," he told her at last. "Think of as a larger version of one of your English country estates. Until recently, my homeland has had little contact with the rest of Europe. I've got a million plans for improving the place, but then so had my father. And my elder brother—to begin with. I'm going to stop the rot. As you insist you're coming to my subject cold, I'll run my ideas past you, as an independent observer. Your job is to spot any flaws."

It was obvious he didn't expect her to find any. His jaw was set, and his dark eyes were resolute. Sara felt a twinge of uncertainty. It would be hard to concentrate with him looking at her like this, but she loved the sound of the challenge he was sending her. "Go ahead." She ran her fingers up and down the cold column of her glass, hoping the condensation would cool her rising temperature. "If we work well together tonight, maybe you'd consider employing my firm to oversee your improvements?"

The waiter arrived with their first course. While it was being served, Leo toyed with the knife lying across his side plate. Sara watched his long sensitive fingers. They were designed for running over those piano keys...or for chasing the shiver that coursed up and down her spine whenever he was near.

"That's the first hurdle I have to overcome. My father had people—or in his case, henchmen—to take care of the day-to-day running of things. When my brother took over, he tried to shoulder all the responsibility, but with limited success. I'm going all the way." His choice of words almost caused Sara to choke on her drink, but he was too busy thanking the waiter to notice.

"Apparently, my staff have already engaged a PR firm to help drag everyone at home into this century, but there's some sort of problem with the arrangements," he said, beginning his meal. "I'm not expected to bother myself with that side of things, but the first thing I'm going to do is put a stop to 'jobs for the boys.'"

Sara was impressed. "I can't see anyone having a problem with that."

"You think so? The problem is, my younger brother is in charge of security. Athan is the man I trust to share my vision, but I can't have one rule for myself, and another rule for everyone else."

"Is your brother any good at his job?"

"He's the best in the business, and everyone knows it." There was a rich undercurrent of pride in Leo's voice. Sara wondered how it felt to have someone like him on her side.

"Then your brother can be the example you hold up to everyone else. Give them performance-related incentives."

He winced at the jargon, and she giggled. "You're paying for my advice, so I have to make it sound official! Make sure you come down hard on your brother if he steps out of line. Treat him the same way you'd treat anyone else."

Her reply seemed to please him. He didn't speak again until their starters had been cleared away.

Resting his elbows on the table, he tapped his fingers against his lips a couple of times before clearing his throat. "You're discreet?"

"I'm famous for it."

"Then I'll tell you something in strictest confidence. It must never go any further, Sara." His dark eyes drove their way into the core of her being with the intensity of diamond-tipped drills. "Loyalty to my heritage stops me returning to England to complete my medical training. Athan's by far the better man to take control at home."

"Why so modest, all of a sudden? You strike me as the sort of guy who could turn his hand to anything."

"I can, but running a country needs a natural leader with the killer instinct. I can't go against my instincts, and 'he did his best' isn't going to cut it for this job."

Sara goggled. "I thought you ran an estate, not a country?"

Leo muttered something under his breath that she couldn't quite catch. Then his lips drew back in a snarl. "I'm laying my life bare, and you pick up on a slip of the tongue?"

She refused to be put off. "The most important part of my job is listening to people, so they get exactly what they want. I'm interested in solving people's problems, not networking over expense-account dinners. The board of directors at ACS is full of Savile Row suits at the moment. What it needs is someone who sees clients as people, not just names on a database and an invoice."

"And you are that person."

"Yes," she said, before realizing he'd made a statement and not asked a question. "So step down in favor of your brother. Other people do it."

"I'm not 'other people.' I am—" He stopped, then fussed with his jacket and tugged down his sleeves in a shameless bit of displacement activity. "It's not an option I can choose. It would never work anyway."

"Then why mention it in the first place?"

He stared at her in disbelief. When she didn't respond, his smile came back. "Because I expect you to come up with a workable alternative, as it's too insane a concept to broach with the people concerned."

"You want my advice? I've given it. Palm your family business off onto your smart-ass brother straight away, and let him sort the problem out."

Leo frowned. "The job was entrusted to me, not him. In any case, Athan enjoys his own job too much to want mine. Our current regime gives him all the excitement he wants without having to get involved with the paperwork, as he puts it."

"Man of action, is he?"

"You could say that. I leave him to do all the flashy, cut and thrust stuff."

"You're a bit of a hero yourself, don't forget." The waiter arrived to clear their table. "That's why dinner is on me tonight," she said. "It's to make up for your impromptu swim earlier on."

His eyes opened wide with surprise. "In my country, women never pay for their own dinner."

Sara frowned. "Hey ho. I can see this relationship is going to take some work."

He put up his hands. "I never mix business with pleasure, and I don't do relationships. I've already told you that."

She tutted her disgust. "A typical male reaction to an innocent remark. I was talking about our business relationship. It was you who put a sexual spin on it."

"Sexual spin? Hmm..."

Temptation flared in his eyes, and her body warmed. Careful not to let it show, she gave him a silent, penetrating stare.

"Very well, Miss Astley. I'll restrain myself, if you'll agree to stop using corporate newspeak."

"So no mention of 'low hanging fruit' then?"

"Not unless you want me to throw you back into the bay." Leo savoured his wine, regarding her over the rim of the glass. Placing it on the table, he eased it out of the way before putting his elbows on the table again. "So...what drew you to party planning?"

Sara gave him a stern look. "I'm in the concierge business, Leo, which is more project planning. I make other people's lives run smoothly," she said, wishing her own life ran as well as her professional work.

"That, if you don't mind me saying so, is far too ordinary a job for a woman like you."

"That's why I do it. My clients are the important

ones, not me. Apis Concierge Solutions attracts them by its reputation. When I take charge, they soon find out how hard I work behind the scenes to give them their heart's desire."

"Does that refer to your private life, as well as your business interests?"

It was exactly the sort of question Sara had been praying he wouldn't ask. "That depends."

"On what?"

"On how I'm feeling at the time."

"Or possibly who?"

"Like you, I never mix business with pleasure." She managed to sound firm, but it was a resolution as wobbly as whipped cream when she looked into Leo's come-to-bed eyes.

"I'm glad to hear it." Leo smiled. "Although I find working with someone is a guaranteed passion killer. That's why I never do business unless it's with someone I like for other reasons." His fingers ran down over the stem of his wine glass to lie in golden relief on the snowy-white tablecloth. They were so close to hers, Sara felt the warmth of him. It radiated from his skin, and smoldered in the depths of his eyes.

"And I love my work." Her words were no longer rigid with conviction.

"You love it so much, I've heard your booking in this hotel is open-ended."

"I didn't make the reservation, so I can't comment. Who told you that?"

"Nick, the owner. Krisia tried to book the suite you're in, and was told Apis Concierge Solutions has it on a long lease."

"Then I was right." Sara congratulated herself, the

report already half-written in her head. "I knew there had to be a reason why they sent me here in particular. They must be thinking about making the Paradise one of our recommended venues. I can use my stay here to produce an in-depth report on the place."

Leo watched her with a mixture of amusement and annoyance. "Do you honestly think medical leave would be a ruse to get you to do more work? Wouldn't your bosses have simply told you to come and study the place?" His expression softened to real concern. "Own up. Maybe you really are here for your own good. Why do you find that so difficult to accept?"

He was back in medic mode. Sara drew her hand well away from his. "I suppose you're right," she said. "I have been throwing myself into my work even more than usual."

"Why?"

"No reason you need bother about." She gave him a smile to soften her words, but that didn't alter her resolve. She still had a lot of hurt to get over before she opened up to a man again.

"Let me guess. Stress and overwork have sucked you dry." His voice was smooth and encouraging.

Sara was so busy trying to decide whether to tell him more about herself, she didn't notice his hand reaching out to her across the table until he drew a caress over her knuckles.

His touch felt as good as he looked. Sara knew she ought to pull away, but it had been so long since anyone had tried to comfort her.

And it's only our hands touching, she thought. That's nothing.

Chapter Five

It didn't feel like nothing. The sensation developing deep inside her whenever she looked at Leo was something she had to laugh about, or she'd end up crying. She knew it. "Damn. I thought my secret was safe," she tried, but her voice shook.

"You have no reason to keep secrets. As the song says, you look perfect to me. Music never lies."

He took her hand and lifted it to his lips. The kiss touched her fingertips and vanished before she had time to think. "If you had a euro for every woman who's fallen for your fibs, I bet you wouldn't have to work for a living." She tried to sound sarcastic but the low, husky quality of her voice ruined that plan.

"I'd never call what I do work." Leo's eyes glittered. He still had hold of her hand, and his smile was fixed. "It's more a lifestyle thing."

"It sounds like we're in much the same business, Leo. Don't tell me you do eighteen-hour days too, at the beck and call of a willful public?"

"That sounds more like a shift in A&E. I'd rather work there than sit around doing nothing and lording it over a horde of minions."

Sara stopped smiling and detached herself from his hand. "I hate delegating work too. I'd rather see a job through alone, from beginning to end."

"That's what I had in mind when I escaped from

home and went away to university in London. I was determined to make an independent life for myself then, and I'm looking forward to doing it a second time."

Sara blinked at the unexpected edge to his voice. A muscle tensed along the smooth plane of his jaw. "That's why I think you'll always be a doctor at heart, Leo. You hate the job you do now, don't you?"

He turned an enigmatic gaze on her. "Whatever else I might say to you, Sara, that's one thing you'll never hear from me."

She said nothing for a minute, then sighed. "That's what I call loyalty. I used to wish I had a close family like yours. It was always just Mom and me. Now I'm on my own. Keep telling me about the downside, about how you had to kill your dreams to keep your family firm afloat, and maybe you'll persuade me I haven't missed out after all."

"I haven't killed anything. A sense of tradition is important."

Sara made a wry face. "I used to think that about marriage, until I met a man who almost got me to the starting gate. Then I saw sense, and gave him his marching orders."

"It's a woman's prerogative."

"That's why I'm a free spirit now. If and when I ever give in to temptation, it'll be marriage or nothing for me."

He was unimpressed. "That's too extreme. You're cutting yourself off from so many subtle gradations of pleasure. Flirting by candlelight, for example." He sat back as the waiter brought the dessert menu. "You can only blow the final whistle when you've tried playing the game. The whole point of coming here on holiday is to leave everyday concerns behind. Go off duty for once, Sara. Who'll know if your icy exterior melts a little in this beautiful Grecian heat?"

His whisper made the candle flames dance. They reignited the cinders of need deep inside Sara's body. As they glowed again, heat rose through her body. "I will. I'll know."

Her words were supposed to warn him off. Instead, they came out sounding like a dare. She watched Leo rise to the challenge. His whole body moved like a predatory animal, and he gave her a smile confirming her fears. Resistance would be useless.

"Ah, you're saying that because you need time to adjust to all this rest and relaxation. Right now you're tense, and still too ready to overreact to every situation. A few days at the Paradise will loosen you up. Then you'll be more...willing to expand your horizons."

"My horizons don't need expanding, thanks. I have my work."

"Yes, you've told me. But with respect, isn't that why you're here? Working too hard?"

"It's how I earned this break."

Leo pursed his lips. "Good catch. I can see you don't let up for a minute."

She allowed herself a small smirk. "As you say, it's what got me here today."

"Laid up on a rest cure."

"You're not actually a doctor, remember."

"When it comes to understanding women, Sara, the only qualification needed is the right set of chromosomes."

Sara gasped at his arrogance. "Now there you're wrong, Mr. Smart-Ass. Sending me flowers was an inspired way to get round your horror of being invited to dinner by a woman. I was touched. But that doesn't mean you, or any of the other men I know, understand me at all."

Leo studied her with a look that was a million miles away from the flirtation usually dancing in his eyes. "You don't strike me as the sort of woman to have got through many lovers, Sara."

She felt a prickle of indignation turn her face red. "I haven't, and that isn't what I said." While Leo studied the dessert menu with interest, Sara left hers on the table. "I haven't had time for a string of lovers. To get where I am today I've had to fight all my life, every inch of the way. That hasn't left me any time for casual affairs."

He leveled a severe look at her. "Kick back. Your doctor's orders, remember? Chill out and indulge yourself for once. With one of these delicious desserts, I mean," he added wickedly.

"I can't. I'll get indigestion."

The professional in Leo rose to that. He gave the waiter an order for two dishes of Sorbet Royale, and waited for Sara to argue. She didn't. When they were alone again, he fixed her with an intense stare. "Twenty-something's shouldn't be getting indigestion."

"I do when I'm stressed."

He raised his eyes to the heavens. "You're on holiday, sitting in this hotel's finest restaurant in the middle of a stunning spa complex and you're telling me you're stressed?"

Sara wriggled in her seat. "Okay. You win. See my face? Take note. This is the nearest I can manage to a sheepish expression."

To her bewilderment, when the waiter arrived with dessert, Leo pushed back his chair and stood up. "You're a ball of tension, Sara. You're winding yourself up tighter and tighter. One day you'll be so wound up, you'll snap. Addiction, depression, suicide…I've seen it all."

"I suppose you've got the ideal prescription?"

He strolled around to stand beside her. "Of course I have. Close your eyes."

"In a public place?" she gasped, but he was serious.

"Do it. Close your eyes and open your mouth." His commanding voice made her obey.

When she realized what she had done, her eyes flew open again—at the exact moment the cool kiss of silver touched her bottom lip. Leo had piled a spoon with champagne granita, and was about to put it into her mouth. "Open wide."

"I'm not a child."

A bead of sorbet fell from the overloaded spoon. It landed on the smooth pale skin at the base of her throat, trembled, then ran down into the shadowy cleft between her breasts. "I can see that," he purred.

"People are staring!"

"Let them. Open your mouth, or—"

"Or—" Or what, she had been going to say, but as she started to reply Leo took his chance. She couldn't talk with her mouth full of sorbet and silver spoon, so she clenched her teeth on it.

"I thought you said you weren't a child?" he teased.

She released her grip on the spoon. "I did that because I've got a chill in my teeth."

"Excuses." He scooped up another helping of the

dessert in front of her. "I'm including a sample of each different flavor, and if you don't enjoy it, well, I'm afraid there's no hope for you."

"Is that your professional opinion?"

"Maybe. First, I'd need to make a full examination..."

She scowled.

"...of the facts. Or something more interesting?" he added, slicing into another scoop of sorbet.

He was concentrating so intently, it was hard not to crack a smile. To resist the impulse, she opened her mouth like a baby bird, ready for the next spoonful.

"On the other hand, perhaps you'd prefer to seek a second opinion," he said, at the very last moment diverting the next scoop of dessert into his own mouth. Sara was left sitting with her mouth open.

"Hey!" Reaching out, she retrieved the spoon and dish from him. Their hands connected, and he laughed. For one heart-stopping moment, his warm fingers sandwiched hers against the cold porcelain of her dish.

There was a question framed in his eyes, and she knew what it was. She looked away, unable to let him guess her answer. She had been fighting temptation from the moment he carried her up the beach, and she wasn't about to stop now.

"You're on holiday, Sara. Loosen up."

His brutal words brought that dark, dangerous night on the road back to her in a horrible rush. The shock of waking as her car veered over the studs at the edge of the carriageway, with just enough time to think she might be about to die as her car hurtled down an embankment before coming to rest in a farmer's field...

Leo's hand went to her mouth, and she realized she

was biting her nails. She stopped before he could tempt her with his touch again. "Oh, I can see danger, all right. It's standing right next to me, Leo."

"Fine. At least I'm an honest threat. Everything about you, from your beautiful appearance to your delightful conversation, your charm and intelligence promises everything any one could want. Why are you so dead set against allowing any man to take what you have to offer?"

"Because that's all they do. Take," she said.

He refused to be put off. "Not me. Where would be the fun in treating a woman like that? I like to give as well as take. You'll see."

"I don't think so. Once bitten, twice shy, remember."

"Don't give me that, Sara. You need to let go, and live a little."

"That laid-back attitude can't have helped your plans to become a doctor," she snipped, but he was more than equal to the challenge.

"It had its advantages, now and again. Unlike my current occupation."

"Whatever that might be, I'm sure your bedside manner comes in useful all the time."

His eyes flashed. Until then, Sara hadn't been too bothered about the job he was concealing. She went very still. "You worry me. Why are you being so secretive about what you do for a living? It makes me think it's either illegal, immoral, or both. Which is it?"

He went back to his seat. As he slumped into it, the candle flames shivered. "Neither. It's the complete opposite, in fact." He stared down at his clasped hands. The waiters cleared their table, then brought coffee and a plate of jewel-like petit fours. Once Leo and Sara were alone again, he lifted his head and leveled a dark, turbulent gaze at her. "I'm in the diplomacy business. Let's leave it at that."

Sara wanted to believe him, but she had to be sure. Fixing him with a stare, she waited. He continued to look into her eyes with an open, almost defiant air.

She was the first to blink. Selecting a tiny tartlet from the plate of petit fours, she made a great show of lifting off the alpine strawberry balanced on top. She saved that to enjoy after she had nibbled through the pastry and creme patissiere confection. "Fine... although I'm not sure where it leaves us."

He relaxed enough to lift the cafetière and pour her a coffee. "I'll still be heading for the mainland tomorrow. And I'm going to insist you come with me."

Sara gave him a sharp, quizzical look. "Is that the man, or the doctor talking?"

"Both. Here's a useful phrase I picked up when I lived in England: 'A little of what you fancy does you good.'" His mouth twitched. The movement drew Sara's gaze to his lips. They had a hypnotic effect. When they moved now it was in a way that drew a tiny sigh from deep down inside her.

"I can't wait to get back home to work," she said, out of habit.

"Then I'll give you a good reason to stay here. You need something to keep your body occupied, as well as your mind." His melodious voice was a silken distraction, matching the irresistible temptation in his eyes. "Let's hope our day out tomorrow satisfies us both, and makes the time you spend here less of a life sentence." The corners of his mouth lifted with dry humor.

The effort of erecting barriers made Sara weary. Why was she fighting so hard? Why not give in, for once?

She leaned toward Leo, mirroring his movements. "That would be perfect."

He signaled to the nearest waiter. "A bottle of your finest champagne, please."

"Although I shouldn't like you to get the wrong idea about me." The Dom Perignon foamed. Once their glasses were filled and the champagne bottle placed in its ice bucket, the waiter made himself scarce. "I'm a smart woman, Mr. Gregoryan. Don't think you can change my mind, whether by fair means or foul," she said, raising her glass in a toast.

"Stinygiasou." He touched his champagne flute to hers with a ring of fine lead crystal. "Spending a day chilling out together would be perfect."

Sara enjoyed her champagne, then put down her empty glass and stood up. "In that case," she said, the ripples of her silvery gown glittering with every movement, "if we're going to get an early start for our trip to the mainland tomorrow I'd better say good night now, Mr. Gregoryan. "

Sara ran up one flight of steps, then gave in and stopped. While she caught her breath, she took off her sandals. The cold marble of the staircase revived her feet, but couldn't cool her passion. Her need for Leo Gregoryan was growing by the second. She wanted him with a primitive, burning lust that consumed her whole body. He played havoc with her common sense, but she had to resist. The moment men took control, they changed.

If I want to save my sanity, I've got to play it cool.

The rational part of Sara's brain was being derailed by her overwhelming need for Leo. Her wits needed a chance to regroup.

This mad, desperate feeling would pass. It had to. Her body wanted to melt through the iron grip of her resistance and reform itself around that infuriating man, but there was no way she could allow that.

She pounded on up the stairs, trying to drive resistance through her body. She needed a cold shower.

With a gasp she ran up the last few steps to her floor, and pushed through the fire door to reach the landing. Head down, she searched in her bag for her key card. Her silent, empty suite was the sanctuary she needed. The crazy jigsaw of her life was missing quite a few pieces, but no search was ever helped by other people piling in.

As she found her key, a sensation she'd never experienced before suffused her body. She looked up. Leo Gregoryan was leaning against the door to her suite.

"Sara..." he drawled, "what took you so long?"

"I was following doctor's orders"—she patted the slight bulge made by the pedometer on her hip—"you'll be pleased to know."

With a smile, he took her hand and pressed it to his lips in the way she loved. The sensation shot a pulse of red-hot need straight up her arm.

"I thought we weren't meeting again until tomorrow morning?"

He twisted his wrist so she could see his watch. Its display had been changed to show eight a.m. the following day.

She half smiled. "Time flies."

"It'll go faster still with me in control," he purred.

Control. There was that word again. The hair on the back of her neck prickled. There were discreet panic buttons everywhere around the hotel. She edged toward the nearest one, but Leo didn't miss a trick. "Hmm. Did I hit a nerve there?"

She contemplated lying to him. With any other man she might have managed it, but Leo's scrutiny was too intense. Without taking her key from her bag, she zipped it shut. Transferring it to her left hand, she took one of her sandals in her right hand. Holding it by the shank so the stiletto pointed toward the floor, she braced herself. "My last partner had strong opinions, and a simple way of expressing them."

"I'm famous for my versatility," Leo said, looking down at the shoe she grasped. "Careful. You could do someone a serious injury with that."

"That's the idea."

He pushed himself upright, then stilled as panic rose in her face. "You won't need it. Not with me."

"I'll be the judge of that."

He lifted his shoulders, and let them fall. "Okay. I can take a hint. Bye, then. Until tomorrow…"

"No—Leo, wait," she said as he moved. She owed him an explanation, if nothing else. "I…don't have the nerve to try again. Yet."

"I'd say it took some nerve to arm yourself, when you could have turned tail and run back down those stairs, Sara."

She pursed her lips, not sure whether to laugh or cry. "After climbing six flights, I'm in no fit state to run anywhere."

He put his head on one side, encouraging her to smile. "I may be many things, Sara, but a bully, I am not." He spread his arms wide. "If you want me, come and get me. Any time. No strings. It's as simple as that."

It would have been the easiest thing in the world to melt into his arms. Sara had been stone-cold sober the last time she made that sort of mistake, and aching with shame and disappointed hopes. Tonight, she was the wrong side of a gourmet meal, one Cinderella, and a straight glass of champagne. To refuse a drop-dead gorgeous guy in a dinner suit on top of that would take some doing. She couldn't throw away her independence, for the sake of releasing all the sexual frustration built up over the past months. Sara was sure Leo would be worth it, but she wasn't about to make any decisions while her blood was running hot and fast through her veins.

"I'll meet you in the foyer tomorrow as arranged, and not before." She pulled out her key card with a flourish. She advanced toward the door of her suite in a way that showed she meant business. With a diplomatic nod, Leo stood aside.

"I'm looking forward to it," she blushed, then added, "seeing your boat, that is."

Leo was intrigued. No woman had ever refused him before. Sara's novelty value meant he could forgive her anything, for the moment at least. He had already swallowed one painful mistake in silence.

His Neroli was a yacht. Not a boat.

To correct her would have been petty. It would also have stopped her shutting the door in his face, but Leo believed in playing a long game. He had right on his side, but Sara's fury would have extinguished the mischievous twinkle in her beautiful hazel eyes. Keeping it alive was worth more to him than proving a point.

Leo thought about that, and all the other delectable parts of her body for a long time. The woman was a delicious distraction. For months, all his thoughts had been black shadows circling the crown of Kharova. Now a stunning creature with more intelligence than his entire entourage of gold-digging airheads put together had pushed them aside. Sara made his immediate future feel a lot more interesting.

He couldn't think of a better way of thanking her than by taking her to his bed. Casual fornication was something the royal and ancient line of Kharova was supposed to resist at all costs.

But then, rules were made to be broken. And Leo was an expert in that department…

Chapter Six

As soon as she was inside her suite, Sara deadlocked the door. Not because she didn't trust Leo, but because she didn't trust herself. The heavy fragrance of lilies reached out to her, and she remembered how her evening began. Leo could never have guessed how the news of that bouquet would touch her. She switched on the lights. The flowers were as beautiful as his gesture. She went over to enjoy them, and touched a petal to make sure it wouldn't disappear in a puff of fantasy.

Leo's appeal didn't lie in looks alone. The way he was charming himself into her life must mean he really did want her.

Sara wanted him too, but she didn't trust herself to take what he was offering. Yet.

There was an envelope on the table, beside the vase of flowers. Picking it up, she grabbed the nearest chair and shoved it against the door of her suite. The more obstacles she could put in the way of her desire to let Leo spoil her, the better. Then she dropped into the seat, and looked at the envelope. It had an English postmark. She flipped it over to see the return instructions. It was from the head office of ACS. It must be official confirmation of her promotion.

With a gasp, she ripped open the envelope and pulled out a sheet of watermarked A4. She had plans for this. The minute she got home, she'd have it framed. It would hang in her bedroom to be the last thing she saw when she went to bed each night, and the first thing to greet her when she woke every morning. It was the official stamp on all her hard work so far, and her inspiration for the future.

She unfolded the letter. With a twinge of satisfaction she saw Ryan, CEO of ACS, had handwritten it himself. She read.

Dear Sara,

I must thank you for the outstanding work you've done for ACS over the past five years. Your contribution has helped us take our place in the vanguard of lifestyle marketing.

I'm writing to inform you of a change to our management structure. As you know, Aidan's departure left a vacancy on the board. Jason has volunteered to step up to the plate.

This means he'll be taking full responsibility for the Kharovan project. You'll be aware we were in danger of losing the contract because of their preference for a male facilitator. Bringing Jason in will smooth the way forward...

Sara folded the piece of paper and slipped it into its envelope. Then she pulled back her arm, and threw the letter as hard as she could. It bounced off the opposite wall, and hit the floor.

Its message had the same effect on her dreams of making a success of the restructuring in Kharova. If ACS thought Jason could cope with the stellar new project she'd wanted, he must have bewitched the entire board. A whole country needed advice. It was a far bigger job than ACS had accepted before, and Sara knew they'd landed the contract because they were cheap. She'd wanted to prove that cutting costs didn't mean sacrificing quality. She knew she could get the one-horse country of Kharova on the road to modernity before Jason and the little country's snooty chamberlain reached the nineteenth hole.

Men. They were all the same. Happy to grab what they wanted, take advantage of her good nature, then trample all over her. Leo had the nerve to look offended when she'd told him as much, but then he knew all about jobs for the boys.

She put her head in her hands. The unfairness of it all set inside her like concrete. The members of the ACS board had caved in to a bunch of backwoods bigots rather than give her time to win the clients around. She imagined her fingers closing around their perma-tanned throats. They'd been so cheerful when they waved her off on this break. Now she knew why. They wanted her out of the way while they cooked all this up. It made her feel sick.

The worst part was, Sara knew that if she wanted to carry on working at ACS she'd have to suck up this disappointment like bitter medicine, and say nothing.

She woke next morning in desperate need of distraction. Putting ACS first hadn't got her anywhere, so she wouldn't waste another minute of her holiday worrying about them. After coffee and fruit overlooking the Aegean, she showered and dressed ready for her day out. A white top, cutoffs, and sandals said cute, but no pushover.

Then she went to see if Leo Gregoryan was as good as she remembered.

He was. Dressed in a white T-shirt and jeans, his clothes were understated, and his tan was healthy. He looked every inch the rich playboy. Languishing on one of the squashy sofas ranged around the foyer, he was looking at a copy of the latest edition of Forbes. He tossed the magazine aside the second she reached the bottom of the stairs, and stood. Hooking his thumbs into his belt loops, he watched her walk toward him.

"I'm sorry about last night," she said before he could speak.

"I know." The slight movement of his head almost persuaded her he did understand. "That's why we'll say no more about it. Let's look on today's expedition as a fresh start. Shall we go?"

He extended his hand to the great glass doors of the Paradise Hotel. They swung open as a gleaming metallic blue saloon prowled up outside. Leo tipped the valet who'd driven it around from the parking area, then held open the passenger door for her.

Sara was about to get in when a sixth sense made her look back at the hotel. Someone was looking at them from an upstairs window. "That's the man I saw picking up Krisia's organizer," she said.

"Where?" Leo asked, looking up at the hotel.

"There... Oh, he's gone. He was at that window, I think." She pointed.

Leo nodded, got out his phone, and spoke a few terse words into it. "No worries," he said.

"This is what I call a car," Sara said, after they'd been driving for a few minutes. "Although there doesn't seem to be much room for supplies."

"The catering party has gone on ahead. I could see you were apprehensive about eating aboard the Neroli, so I told them to wait on the mainland for my instructions."

Sara let her breath go in a rush. Not having to worry about eating while she was at sea was a huge relief.

Her experiences of being a passenger driven by high-powered clients with more testosterone than brain cells meant Sara had been tense as she got into Leo's car. Hiding her hands, she'd clutched the edge of her seat to begin with, but he had nothing to prove. He was a fast driver, but safe. The knots in the muscles of her neck and shoulders soon untangled, and by the time they reached the harbor, she was relaxed enough to take a risk with him.

"I've been thinking about what you said last night, Leo. About working with someone being the perfect passion killer."

He drew back his lips in a tigerish grin. "It works every time, in my experience."

"The fact is, I don't need any more complications in my life, but I've reached a bit of a crossroads as ACS has turned its back on me."

"I thought you were expecting a promotion. They've sacked you instead?"

"Worse. They've given my ex the position I should have had. All because the client they're brown-nosing doesn't believe in letting a woman handle their business—the fat-headed, peanut-brained dinosaurs," she told him. "Men like that want to keep women barefoot, pregnant, and chained to the kitchen sink. Every one of them who thinks like that should be hanged, drawn, and quartered."

Leo frowned. "When you rant like that, you're

giving them more ammunition."

Sara had expected a man who solved problems with flowers to be fawning around her, full of sympathy. His hard-faced irritation was a shock.

"Don't say that means you think women are good for nothing else too?" she snapped.

"No, but I've got no time for anyone—male or female—who makes sweeping generalizations."

"How can you sit there and say that? You might as well take their side!"

"I don't take anyone's side until I know all the facts." His mouth was a grim line as he concentrated on the road ahead.

"Some tin-pot dictator tells them he'll only deal with men, so they roll over and parachute in a guy who's all talk and no action?"

"It sounds like your ex will be the perfect man for the job in a place like that. In my country, men are the diplomats while women are the managers. They oil the wheels of society and keep things running, while men do the steering and operate the brakes." He swung into a parking space on the sea front.

"Then I hope their feet aren't rusted to the pedals, like the misogynists in Kharova," she snorted.

Leo wrenched on the handbrake and scowled at her. "That's who you were going to be working for?"

"I thought it would be a challenge. I suppose I should call it a narrow escape, and be glad I won't have to pander to them."

"You? Pander to anyone who doesn't share your vision of the perfect world? I don't think so." He sounded bitter.

"ACS must have ganged up with my PA and my

doctor to get me out of the way while Jason wormed into my place," she went on.

"Now that's paranoia, Sara. You're so stressed out, going straight back into that high-pressure environment would be the worst thing you could do. And that's my private opinion, as well as a professional one."

Sara fumed as he got out of the car and walked around to open the passenger door for her.

"The great and good at Apis Concierge Solutions have made their biggest mistake yet, Sara," he said as she got out. "They've underestimated you."

"Underestimated, undervalued—you name it, they've done it," she muttered.

"Including awarding that promotion to your greatest rival?" His voice was measured. He could see Sara was furious with herself as well as ACS, for letting the firm take advantage of her. It made her so mad, she didn't bother to hide her feelings. She bit the side of her nail. "Yes."

Leo took her hand away from her mouth, and used his hold on her to escort her along the dock. A smart blue-and-silver speedboat was moored there for them, complete with pilot. Handing her down into the craft, Leo waited until they were well away from the jetty before speaking.

"You know that discussion we had last night?" he called, the breeze whipping his words away, "Why not tell ACS where to stick their job? Come and work for me. I've already told you I'm restructuring my team. After what ACS has done to you, leaving them would be the perfect revenge."

Sara held on tight to a grab-handle as the speedboat bucked over the open water between the harbor and the

Neroli. She considered her reply until the vessel made a graceful arc to come alongside the beautiful yacht. "Thanks, Leo, but unlike the board of ACS, I know what the word loyalty means. I've got regular clients I love to work with."

"Of course," he said with grudging respect. "It's not a good idea to make a snap decision at a time like this. But how about trying a little freelancing for me here, while you're on holiday?"

"I'm not sure... I'd have to let ACS know what I was doing, or I couldn't live with myself."

He smiled, but without humour. "I'm glad to hear it. How much longer do you want to stay at the Paradise?"

"It'll be a while, given the way I feel right now."

"Good."

The speedboat idled to a stop. Once Leo had helped her aboard his yacht, Sara put her hand up to shield her eyes and gazed back at Paradise Island. The glittering white walls and broken red roofline of the hotel and spa complex shimmered like a mirage in the distance. It looked like heaven, and it was a place she would never have experienced for herself if it hadn't been for ACS. She didn't want to lose that luxury, but she didn't want to be forever in the debt of her employer, either. If she made a good job of working for Leo, it would prove she could fly her career solo.

"In which case, name your price, Sara," he said, breaking into her thoughts as he took the wheel to steer the Neroli out into the bay.

She took in a few deep, refreshing breaths of sea air before she answered him. "I'll take the going rate, Leo. Job satisfaction means more to me than money."

"Really?"

The way he lingered over the word made her wonder. "What's the matter? I can't be the first person who's said that to you!"

"Yes, you are. I can't tell you how good it is to find a woman who's more interested in me than in my bank account." His smile was genuine as he let the wheel of the Neroli run through his hands.

Sara sat with her back to the rail. When they met in the foyer she'd been half-afraid he would take up where he'd left off the night before. That would have thrown her into confusion again, wanting him and yet not ready to risk the pain closeness to another person could bring.

Instead, Leo was the perfect host. Sara knew she should be glad. He set a course for the headland and sailed the vessel around it, sending white spray knifing up from its prow. He was so at one with the streamlined beauty of his yacht, it was impossible not to want him. The fierce, primitive desire provoked by a man at the top of his game almost overwhelmed her.

"I'm too busy managing my own finances to care about other people's," Sara threw her words into the wind. "You can thank my mother for that. One of her favourite sayings was 'When you've got a pound, you've got a friend.' We had precious few 'friends' when I was a child, so the moment I was old enough I got a job. I've worked to pay my own way ever since."

"So you don't define yourself by the kind of guys you date?" He was surprised.

She blew her fringe out of her eyes in exasperation. "If I did, I'd never be able to get out of bed in the morning."

That made Leo think. In his opinion, Sara Astley

shouldn't be allowed out of bed without a bodyguard, anyway. "That good, eh?" he chuckled.

"Quite the opposite. Maybe I should have said, I'd never be able to look my reflection in the eye. To use another of my mom's catchphrases, I can't half pick them, Leo."

That was one problem Leo didn't have. "Bimbos are always hitting on me. I'm immune, but it's partly why I keep a low profile."

"Of course. Someone in your position must have standards to maintain."

Leo sent up a silent prayer of thanks. At last, a woman who could appreciate his problems without mentioning the dreaded crown-shaped elephant in his robing room. He felt safe in returning her smile.

"I'm glad you see it that way, Sara. You're one of the few people who do. I like a woman with subtlety."

"And I find there's nothing like a self-effacing man." She was smiling.

Leo congratulated himself as he checked his charts. This was the sort of person he wanted to brighten his last days as a free man.

Sara had been scared she would embarrass herself, and Leo, by being seasick. Instead the sea was so calm, she felt a wonderful sense of release. The Neroli swept across the surface like a swallow. She loved it. "You handle this boat like you were born to it, Leo."

He seemed to find this funny. Seeing him look so happy made her heart do a little dance in her chest. The tousled man who kicked off his shoes and commanded his vessel barefoot and windblown was a world away from the sleek seducer of the night before. "You looked so miserable when you were playing the piano to Krisia in the bar."

"Did I? That's what happens when you let your work interfere with your private life."

Sara had a sudden crisis of conscience. She hadn't texted her PA since the night before. Digging in her bag for her mobile, she switched it on. "Why do I get the funniest feeling I'm being watched?" she asked without looking up from the keypad.

"Because you are. And there are two good reasons for that."

She paused before sending the message. "You're going to moan at me for checking mail when I should be taking a break."

He grinned at her. "That was one of the reasons."

She guessed the other before he put it into words. "Blushing suits you, Sara."

"It'll look a whole lot better when my skin's lost this pasty white colour."

Leo clicked his tongue. "A woman like you should be sophisticated enough to accept compliments with better grace."

"Sorry, but I don't take orders from a guy who looks like a pirate." Switching off her phone, she lolled back against the rail. It felt good to forget work for once, and let the sun pour over her body. "Stop laughing, Leo."

"If I'm a pirate, then the sea should be my only mistress. Is that what you want?" His voice came from much closer than it should. She jumped. He was leaning against the rail now too, so close she could have reached out and touched him.

"Who's sailing the boat?" she asked, alarmed.

"Don't worry," he said. "The Neroli is perfectly

trained, and does as I tell the on-board computer. There's someone on lookout as well. And for the record, my Neroli is a yacht, not a boat."

He was too close for comfort, but with a tingle of fear Sara realized he wasn't close enough for her. She made a derisory noise to cover her confusion. "You'd hand over control to a computer? I work with those things all day, and there's no way I'd trust my life to one of them."

"But you trust me," he said.

"No, I don't. Not one inch."

"Why not, as a matter of interest?"

She gave him a frank look. "Here's a question. How can you tell when a man is lying to a woman?"

He shrugged.

"His mouth is moving."

Her barb hit home, and she enjoyed seeing it happen. At least they both knew where they stood.

"Ouch. I thought you said you'd never met my brother Athan?" he asked with a grimace.

"I haven't. And I've met all the men I want to meet socially, thanks very much."

"Yet you agreed to come out with me today on the Neroli."

"You made it impossible for me to refuse," she said. "And it'll be the perfect chance to test my willpower."

"I wouldn't be so sure about that. As a gentleman, I wouldn't dream of offering you any temptation you wouldn't want." His lips were slightly parted, giving a glimpse of his even white teeth. They made a perfect contrast with the honeyed gold of his tan, and he knew it. This man didn't need to move a muscle to offer her mortal sin on a plate. His body told her all she needed to know, and more.

She was nursing the biggest disappointment she'd ever experienced, and needed to stop it hurting. Sara wanted Leo to take it all away. He cupped the side of her face with his hand. The raw sexuality of his touch played over her skin like fire. She wanted to close her eyes and melt under his touch, but not here. Not in a place where he was in control and there was no possibility of escape. She eased away from him.

"I don't do this any more, Leo."

"Is that you, or your career talking?" His rich, eastern European tones sent a shiver down her spine.

"Both."

"When I was at Eton, my masters warned me all work and no play makes Jack a dull boy."

...and makes Jill a dull lay, Sara recalled. "So you went to Eton, did you? Name dropper!"

Her reaction amused him. "You're the first woman I've met who didn't slaver with interest when I slipped that into the conversation. It's often something to do with money—but not always."

Sara found herself laughing. He was even sexier when he was beside her than when he'd been silhouetted at the wheel.

"You're a real breath of fresh air, Sara."

"And you're a devious, home-wrecking heartbreaker. I thought I'd save time by filling out your charge sheet now, rather than later."

"So you think there's going to be a later, do you?"

"There you go again, Leo, turning my words against me! I can check 'devious' off my list of your coming attractions." Damn! It was the first time she'd let her true feelings show, and she could have kicked herself. She caught her breath in a little cough. "I mean, sins."

"You sound like a woman who tempts fate, but as you're not married I don't qualify as a home wrecker."

"I called you a heartbreaker too," Sara said, expecting him to deny it all without thinking. When he pursed his lips and raised one hand to waggle it, she was suspicious. "What's that supposed to mean?"

"It means I can't help it if I'm irresistible, but as I always choose my women carefully, it doesn't usually happen."

"Usually?" She watched him, hoping to make him spill more details.

He had the grace to look solemn. "After what you said at dinner last night, I asked Krisia if she was in love with me. For some peculiar reason, she said no," he said without a trace of irony.

"It must be your shy, retiring nature!" she laughed.

He nodded. "That may be a part of it."

Sara exploded in a fit of giggles. "Not to mention your self-effacing charm!"

"I don't know about that! She's my second cousin. My HR unit hated it when I took her on, but I overruled them. She's the perfect person to keep me on the straight and narrow. Although to be fair, her qualifications are so good I gave her the choice of becoming my PA, or going for a position with my brother." He stopped, realized what he had said, and grinned. "A legitimate, clerical position, that is."

"And so Krisia chose nice brother over nasty brother."

The amusement went out of his expression, like the

sun going behind a cloud. "Don't speak about Athan like that."

The chill that ran through Sara's body had nothing to do with pleasure this time. She had roused the eagle in him. To prove he hadn't intimidated her, she locked her eyes onto his cold stare. "I don't know the guy so yes, you're right. I shouldn't have jumped to conclusions about him."

The relaxation in his muscles was so slight, if Sara hadn't been watching him minutely she would have missed it. The wild streak in him was satisfied, for now. "My brother is a good man at heart, but when it comes to women he can be...impulsive."

Sara didn't trust herself to guess what that meant. "Then I'm glad I'm sitting on a yacht miles out to sea with you, rather than him."

"So am I." Leo twisted round and slid down to sit beside her. "We understand each other, Sara. You don't trust men, and use your work as a form of escape. I use women as a form of escape, and I don't trust anyone else to do my work for me."

Sara grinned. "Most people don't get that, do they? About nobody else doing things properly? They think it makes you a control freak!"

"Is that what they say about you?" There was no flirtation in Leo's manner now.

"Don't they say it about you too?"

"Never." She watched him reconsider, before he added, "Not to my face, anyway. They wouldn't dare."

Sara could believe that. The transformation she'd seen whenever she overstepped the mark with Leo proved he prized loyalty. Anyone close to him had to be above suspicion. His arm was resting on his knee as he sat beside her. A minor tilt of the yacht, and the tip of his fingers almost brushed her thigh.

His voice jerked her out of a very rude daydream. "Detachment isn't always bad, you know. By keeping women in perspective, I avoid any messy entanglements."

"I'm off men, remember?"

"So you keep saying...but I am no ordinary man."

Watching the sun burnish his bare arms and the wind ruffle his dark curls, she could believe it. Leo was as comfortable with the elements as he had been in the sophisticated surroundings of the Paradise Hotel.

"You're the same as me, Sara. An individualist, who won't let anyone tell them what to think or feel." His voice was the purr in the throat of a lion.

"That includes you, Leo."

He seemed to have more admiration for Sara than she felt for herself. Her willpower was draining away by the second.

"You're showing me a unique experience, Sara. The less you want from me, the more I want from you. It's usually the other way around."

"I think they call it the thrill of the chase."

"I'd find it disappointing if you were the first chaste woman I'd met."

"I'm sure you can do better than that, Leo! Anyway, my last experience of being caught put me off." Planting her hands on the deck she pushed herself away from him again.

"You're determined not to make this easy for me, aren't you?" He chuckled, reaching to brush a strand of her windblown hair back from her face. "I like the way your mind works. But I also like my women one hundred percent willing."

"So?"

"You decide what happens, when the time is right. Until then, let's concentrate on getting to know each other better. Socially."

"Yes," Sara said with a slow smile. "I think that would be a very good idea."

"Tell me, Miss Astley, how far do you think this exchange of pleasantries will go?"

"It might take you as far as you want. Eventually."

"Really? For a woman who has sworn off relationships, isn't that attitude dangerous?"

"This is a definite one-off. You're an intelligent man. I'm a careful woman. I'm sure you don't take risks any more than I do. If we're both adult about the situation, there's no reason why we shouldn't enjoy a simple expedition with no comeback."

Chapter Seven

When they sailed into port on the mainland, men in sinister shades and smart suits were waiting for them. Leo and Sara were escorted to a smart 4x4 for the trip out of town. As they headed northwest, civilization unraveled. Within minutes, they were driving through sunbaked countryside. The land rose, and their surroundings became rougher and lonelier. Although it was still early in the day, Sara felt the heat. Leo handled the vehicle with the same expertise he'd used on the Neroli, and she found that sexy. When they left the main road, the journey got more exciting. Negotiating potholes and rutted tracks, he took them high into the hills until Sara spotted a big spread of low buildings in the distance. Their white walls sparkled like snow against the dry landscape.

"That's our destination." Leo's face was transformed. His look of anticipation made Sara forget the two burly security men sitting behind them. Leo had more charm and skill than all the men she had known, put together. When she told him she didn't do casual sex, it was true—but there was nothing casual about the feelings stirring within her now.

When they reached the farmhouse, staff gave them breakfast then showed them where they could change into riding gear. Close-fitting jodhpurs and boots made Sara feel the part of a rider, although her nerves were jangling at the thought of getting on a horse for the first time. They were eclipsed by her self-consciousness when she met Leo in the yard.

"You look good in that outfit." He nodded appreciatively. Sara could have said the same thing to him, but kept quiet. She had been careful to cover up as much as possible, using the Greek sun as an excuse. Trying to avoid tempting Leo was the real reason. "Are your security men coming with us?"

Leo shook his head. "There's no need. This estate and all the land around it belongs to a trusted friend of mine. It's as secure as anywhere can be. We'll never be out of contact." He patted the bulge of his mobile. "I've spent plenty of time surviving in the wild." As if to prove it, he accepted a rucksack from one of his team.

"A sophisticated guy like you? I'm amazed."

"You don't know the half of it," Leo told her. "There was such an age difference between my eldest brother and the rest of us, we didn't have much to do with him. When we were younger, I was always boss in charge of the others. Before my brother Athan discovered Officer Training, he used to nag me to play soldiers, and teach him woodcraft. It was a big relief to go back to helping our sister with her music, I can tell you."

"I enjoyed your playing last night," she said on impulse.

"Thanks. It's not often I'm appreciated for what I do."

"Honestly, Leo, you say your brother's a live wire, but you can save lives, sail, teach survival skills—is there anything you can't do?"

"No," he said.

Two horses were led out from their stables before Sara could tease him about his self-confidence again. Leo left a groom holding his bay gelding, while he explained the basics of riding to Sara. She hadn't been looking forward to the experience, but Leo assured her the small grey horse chosen for her was very quiet. She steeled herself to give it a try. Once she was in the saddle, the sensation wasn't as bad as she expected, although the ground seemed a long way away.

Leo swung himself up onto his own horse, and led Sara out into the countryside. Her nervousness soon evaporated. "Are you saying the army's not your thing, Leo?"

"Don't get me wrong. It's a wonderful institution, but I spent a long time learning to heal bodies. That isn't what being a soldier is about."

Sara saw him take in a great breath and expel it as a sigh. She couldn't resist putting out her hand to clap him on the back. "Good choice, Leo. If brainwork's more your thing, let others do the swashbuckling."

He agreed. "I'd rather do something like this—help you to recharge your batteries the natural way—than charge about in burnt cork and fatigues. I'm happy to leave that side of things to Athan."

They rode on, through olive groves streaked with fitful shadows. The sun rose higher in the sky. To begin with Sara was too busy admiring the way Leo rode, and trying to copy his style, to talk. As she relaxed she discovered he had hidden depths. He knew the names of all the birds dancing through the branches around them. Now and then he would point out the dry and cracked remains of a wild boar wallow, or the tufts of gingery hair where deer had scratched an itch against the bark of a tree.

When they stopped in the shade of an ancient wild fig tree, she looked at him with new eyes. Despite the baking heat, she felt refreshed.

"It's amazing. I hadn't realized how stiff my neck and shoulder muscles were until this trip gave them the chance to relax. This is better than hours of therapy. It must be why you offer trips like this to people like Mrs. Revere."

"That is a one-off. I'll be far too busy to do anything like it in future." Leo leaped down from his horse to help her dismount.

"Oh, I know the feeling." Sara thought she had riding all worked out. She wasn't ready for the wobble that came when her feet landed on the ground. She gasped, and stumbled. Leo's hands went straight to her waist, helping her regain her balance.

"Which is why you should take better care of yourself." He let her go, but not before patting her with disapproving firmness. "You should eat more. I can count every one of your ribs."

"You shouldn't be looking."

"I was working by touch."

"That's worse."

Pulling the rucksack off his shoulders, he dropped it beneath the wide-spreading boughs of the fig. "Alexander the Great is supposed to have feasted beneath this tree. A frown like yours would have frightened him off." He unbuckled a kilim from behind the saddle of his horse, and asked her to spread it on the ground while he took the animals to drink from a nearby stream. When he came back from tying them in the shade of an olive tree, she was still setting out their meal.

"The Greeks believe in feeding people well." She eyed the amazing number of salads. Each was in its own container, along with cold meats, cheeses, and bottles of mineral water.

"That's one of the reasons I love it here." He dropped onto the rug and stretched out his long legs before helping himself to some feta salad. "How about you?"

Sara couldn't reply. She was torn between drinking in the scenery, with its spicy perfume of wild herbs, and selecting something from the picnic. In the end she chose some marinated mushrooms, a sunflower seed roll and a string of cherry tomatoes. Settling down to enjoy the soundtrack of insects and warblers, she considered her answer. "I was born and brought up in the city. I can't exist without background chatter. My radio goes on the minute I get up, and stays on till I leave the house and plug in my headphones. Sitting under a tree in the middle of nowhere is a new experience for me. I never thought I'd say this, but I'm enjoying myself."

A lack of conversation usually made her uneasy. Today was different. She wanted to ask Leo about his life and work, but didn't say a thing. This was the first time she'd been part of a friendly silence, and she didn't want to disturb it.

"You've lost your ring," he said, and looked ready to radio up a search.

Sara dug a finger into the breast pocket of her borrowed shirt. "Here it is. I took it off."

"Does that mean you feel safe enough with me to drop your pretense?"

She dropped the ring back into its hiding place. Her nails almost went to her mouth, but at the last moment she diverted her hand toward her hair instead. "I don't make the same mistake twice." She twiddled a strand of hair between her fingers, hoping it was true.

"I suppose that's what makes you the perfect concierge."

She searched his expression for sarcasm. Not finding any, she took a sip of water in case he caught her looking smug. "Once a client entrusts me with their project, they don't have to lift a finger. My team organizes everything for them, right down to the smallest detail. Satisfaction guaranteed."

"I can imagine." Leo tugged some pearly green grapes out of a fruit bowl. Tipping his head back, he dropped them into his mouth.

Sara sensed he was about to smile, but she was ready for him. "Imagine all you like. I'm very good at my job." It was what she always told everyone, but somehow today those words didn't fill her with the usual glow of satisfaction. It was odd.

Leo didn't seem to notice anything out of place. "I know you are. If you weren't, I wouldn't have confided in you last night."

Her brow furrowed. "You don't like to tell anyone what's going through your head, do you? When I was sounding off about the women-haters who robbed me, you could see their point of view, couldn't you?"

"Yes, because I grew up in that culture. Our women are treated differently from yours. They have their place in society and don't waste their time heckling men. Instead they care for the sick and elderly, manage the household, and educate the children. Their work is as important as any man's, but at the moment it's done within the household, rather than outside."

Sara roused with fury, but Leo hadn't finished. "I'm going to change that. I want all my people—whether men or women—to look outwards. They should share their knowledge, skills, and expertise beyond their own family circles."

"How many women are employed in top jobs on your estate?"

"None. Yet."

Her mocking laughter was calculated to get under his skin. "Hah! You're as bad as every other man born into a mediaeval culture. It's easy to say you'll change things. I bet there will always be something more important to do first."

Leo had been leaning on one elbow, twirling the sprig from his bunch of grapes. The venom in her voice made him sit up. "It's bad enough when my ambitions have to take second place to someone else's expectations. Now you're accusing me of being callous, because from one conversation you've deduced everything there is to know about my culture? At least we value our women. We don't treat them with the contempt ACS showed you."

Sara stared at him in breathless silence, realizing she'd crossed a line.

"I want to make life better for everyone, without making it worse for anyone," he ground out. "But whatever I do will upset someone. It's a nightmare. You don't think I'm taking on this job for fun, do you?"

Sara released the breath she hadn't known she was holding. "You keep telling me to take advice—your advice, my doctor's advice, my board's advice—so take some yourself. Give it up, Leo!"

"Loyalty is a serious matter. It means a lot to me." He wrenched the lid off a bottle of iced mineral water. He drank, straight from the neck of the bottle.

She watched, feeling the tension draining out of the air. "Leo," she said after a long pause. "About last night... I'm sorry if I gave you the wrong impression."

"So am I. For the first time in my life, my fabled bedside manner didn't get the result I expected."

"It wasn't your fault." Her thumb rubbed against her bare ring finger, ready to twiddle the golden fake. It was another habit she would have to lose, and fast.

The nod he gave her might have passed for understanding, but she got the idea he knew she wasn't telling the whole truth.

He started gathering their picnic things. "Then I'll stop stirring up your inner demons, and concentrate on trying to protect your exterior instead. Did you put on any sunscreen before we set off?"

Sara looked down. She had diverted her nervous fingers to the tingling skin of her wrists. They were red from the sun. "Some, but I wasn't intending to bask. I'm not a lizard."

"Now that, I can see for myself. Let's ride back to civilization before you're burned to a crisp."

...and before I do something I'll regret, Sara thought.

They traveled to the farm buildings in uneasy silence. Sara finally admitted to herself she wanted Leo, on her own terms, or not at all. For her, losing control wasn't an option. The thought of losing it out here in the wilds unnerved her still more.

She couldn't get back to the stables fast enough.

"You've forgotten how to enjoy yourself." Leo helped her down from her horse. "And before you say I've gone to the other extreme, don't forget the sand is running out of my egg-timer of freedom."

"What? What do you mean?"

He gave her a strange look. "You know. What's happening next month..." He gestured with his hand to encourage her to fill in the gap.

"No, I don't know. What are you talking about?"

Leo looked down at a brilliant green damselfly as it settled on his shirt and clung there, glittering like the highlights in Sara's eyes. "Oh, come on! I know you said when we first met that you had no idea who I was, but I assumed you were humoring me..." he said, but she didn't cut in with the confession he expected. "So you've really got no idea what's going on?"

She twisted a lock of her hair. "I only know what you've told me. You're Leo Gregoryan, ex-medical student, otherwise international man of mystery. If the hotel hadn't been issued with instructions to keep me offline I would have checked you out long ago, but as it is..." She shrugged.

It was decision time. Leo set his jaw. If Sara didn't already know he was the as-yet uncrowned King of Kharova, she would change the instant he told her. Women always did. It happened the moment they were formally introduced. He'd watch them calculating his net worth and measuring themselves for the crown of his queen consort. Every time, they were disappointed. Leo never allowed himself to get close to any of them. His father had taken a wife from outside the aristocratic clans of Kharova. Leo wanted to do the same, but it would take a very special woman and all his tact and diplomacy to keep his beloved country onside. His distant relative Mihail wanted the throne. That man had powerful friends, and came from a pure Kharovan bloodline he could trace back for centuries. The job of king was risky enough for someone born to it, who had been trained to recognize the dangers. It had killed both Leo's parents in the end, and Leo didn't intend exposing any woman to the same risk if he could help it.

Sara couldn't know anything about his life in Kharova. She was filling his last few precious hours of freedom with amazing thoughts and desires. He couldn't break this spell by telling her he was heading for his coronation. If he did, she'd be transformed in an instant. She would stop fluttering like a trapped bird, push her shoulders back and her breasts forward, and change from a linnet into a bird of paradise at the drop of a regal title.

It took him so long to decide what to say; his words were hardly more than a gruff whisper. "We've had some good times together, Sara..."

She went pale. "So...it's that sort of bad news. You're dying?" she whispered.

His face twisted with the irony of it. "No. At least, not if I can help it. But you saying that puts things into perspective for me, Sara. You know as much about Leo Gregoryan as you need to. "

The atmosphere between them lightened. His mention of time slipping away galvanized Sara. Whatever lay ahead for Leo, she wanted him to enjoy his last few days of freedom. Her business skills might help him make all the changes he wanted back at his home. Without treating his staff the way ACS treated me, she thought.

The way Leo took the helm of his yacht for their return journey to the island convinced her he wasn't a man to be confined by a desk job. He needed to challenge himself all the time, and those around him. Any woman who tangled with Leo Gregoryan needed to be his equal. Making a success of his new position in life mattered to him. If she could do anything to lift some of the burden from his shoulders, then she would.

With his hard work, dedication, and loyalty, Leo could rule the world if he wanted...

Chapter Eight

Leo rinsed his razor, lined it up alongside the sink and stared at his reflection in the mirror. He'd got more enjoyment out of these last few days than on any other holiday. He looked forward to spending time in Sara's company, like a child waiting for his birthday. It was a strange feeling. He often used women for relaxation, but being with Sara wasn't relaxing. It was like cosying up to a tiger, but less dangerous and more satisfying. Why was she so different? There was a spark, an emotional response to her he'd never felt before. Sara made him feel alive. She was intelligent, too dedicated to her work for her own good—and far more beautiful than she realised.

Lots of women had those qualities, so why did his heart always beat faster at the thought of seeing her? It must be something to do with the way she wouldn't give in. Not to him, but to herself. He had a shrewd idea she was attracted to him as much as he was to her, but she wouldn't let herself enjoy what he was offering. Maybe that was part of her attraction. He could simply enjoy her company without having to put on a show. There was no need for the continuous flirting his usual arm candy expected. Sara was a breath of fresh air, even if it sometimes felt he was walking headfirst into a gale. And he loved every moment of it.

He strolled out of the bathroom and found Krisia

rummaging through his wardrobe. His PA was a different form of wildlife, more a cross between a boa constrictor and a broody hen. Disapproval radiated off her today, spiced with the air of martyrdom. I've learned all that from the set of her shoulders, Leo thought with a grimace. "Krisia—what are you doing?"

"Choosing clothes for your day out with that woman. You might not be taking your responsibilities seriously, Your Majesty—Leo—but I do. You represent Kharova. You should maintain our country's image and reputation."

"Oh, for goodness' sake. I'm on holiday, not chairing a meeting at the UN. And call Sara by her name, please. She's done nothing to upset you. Treat her with some respect."

Krisia sniffed, and turned back to the wardrobe. Pulling open a drawer, she took out some socks. Leo swore under his breath and strode toward her. Snatching the socks from her hands, he pointed at the door. "I'm quite capable of dressing myself, thank you. Go and set up the link to Athan, please."

Leo wasn't easily depressed, but the daily calls with his brother didn't often bring good news these days. Athan, his head of security, was more than capable of dealing with any problems back at home, but it was all ultimately Leo's responsibility.

He had just thrown his robe into the bathroom when the door opened and Krisia appeared again.

"Don't you ever knock?" he bellowed, turning his back on her and pulling on his underpants.

"Don't get so upset. I've seen you naked before," said Krisia. He could hear her grinning, and knew she would be admiring his body. It was what other women did, which was why he didn't like his PA doing it.

"Yes, but we were children then! You were spying on me and my brothers in the river," Leo snapped, doing up his trousers.

"I wasn't spying. My mother told me to make sure you didn't get into trouble."

Leo huffed in exasperation. "And you've been doing that ever since." He pushed her back through the doorway so he could follow her into his drawing room. "Both the spying, and the babysitting."

Leo went to the desk where a monitor was already showing Athan's proud face. He didn't approve of his brother's chaotic personal life, but the man was a machine when it came to his work as head of Kharovan security. Leo respected that. He loved his brother, but with a tinge of envy for some parts of his lifestyle. Putting that aside, he got down to business. "How are things today?"

"Quiet, Your Majesty," his brother replied, grinning.

"Call me that again, and I'll give you such a hiding when I get back," Leo said in a way that made Athan laugh out loud.

"Seriously, it's been quiet. Mihail's been giving the newspapers plenty of copy and there have been a few skirmishes among his followers, but nothing to worry about. Do you want me to crack down on him?"

Leo frowned. He wasn't a stranger to tough decisions, but that didn't make them any easier. King of Kharova wasn't simply a ceremonial role. His people took their monarchy seriously. "If he can get away with letting off hot air, might it encourage him to try harder?"

Athan shrugged. "If it was up to me, I'd have a word with him behind the scenes and tell him to cool it. Nothing official. I'll remind him we've got nothing against free speech, but he's got to keep his supporters under closer control."

"All right. Thank you, Krisia," Leo said as she brought him a cup of coffee and a pastry.

"I don't see why you should put up with Mihail at all," Krisia grumbled. "You're the king, not him. Opposing you means opposing our country. That makes him a traitor."

"No," Leo and his brother said at the same time.

"Mihail is as patriotic as you are," Leo continued. "He sees my plans for our country's future as a threat to Kharova's traditions and way of life. Mihail's clan has always favoured more...explicit ways of putting across their point of view. Our family prefers diplomacy. I'm not going to start my reign with a civil war!"

"You could always marry into his clan," Athan said. "That should keep him quiet."

"I don't think I'll be doing that. If nothing else, it would upset a whole new section of the community. You know the king is supposed to choose a bride from within his own circle." Leo noticed Krisia gazing at him as he said that. When he caught her eye, she blushed.

"Have you decided who you'll marry?" Athan continued, unaware of the bombshell he'd dropped.

"Don't be in such a rush. I'm not even crowned yet! Anyway, no suitable candidate has presented herself." Leo heard a snort, and saw his PA scowl. He waved her away. "Thanks, Krisia, that'll be all. I'll ring if I need anything." He watched until she had left, closing the door behind her. Even her back radiates annoyance, he thought.

Athan cleared his throat. "What about marrying Krisia?"

"Do me a favour. We'd drive each other insane before our first anniversary. Besides, I've never felt that way about her. She's a great PA and puts Kharova before everything, but that's not what I'm looking for in a wife."

"So?"

"It's got to be someone I want to share the rest of my life with—someone who'd be a good mother to my children and a good queen too. With all that entails."

"Fine. I can think of any number of women in our clan who are perfect for that role. They'd jump at the chance."

Leo sighed. "We've been through this often enough. You know I can't have children with one of our own. We've got some very bad genes in our DNA."

"Who said you had to have children with her?"

"What?"

"You said it yourself. Your wife has to be a good mother to your children. Who says they have to be her children?"

Leo was lost for words.

"No one expects our king to be in love with the woman he marries," his brother went on. "It'll be a marriage of political expediency. That's how these things work, and always have done. Marry her, but make your children with someone who's more acceptable to you. That's what I'm going to do, when the time comes. It's what mistresses are for."

Leo could hardly believe what he was hearing. He hadn't realized how cynical and unfeeling Athan could be. Their parents' bad marriage must have taken a toll on him, even though Leo had tried to protect him from the worst moments.

"If you think like that, why don't you marry into Mihail's clan?" he asked, when he'd got over his initial shock.

Athan shrugged. "I'm not king. There's no political benefit in it for either side."

"You mean you've never thought about marrying for love?"

His brother grunted. "No. Why fool yourself? Marrying for love didn't work for our mother and father, did it? Nor for anyone else we know. Accept it for what it is, Leo. A legal agreement. Nothing more. Don't tell me you, of all people, believe in love?"

Leo's mind raced. He avoided thinking about marriage as much as possible. If it crossed his mind, it was in the way Athan described—a political necessity for the sake of Kharova. Now it was dawning on him real life wasn't as easy, or clinical as that. He wanted more than a marriage of mere convenience. He wanted a real wife and a real family, not political pawns. Finding an acceptable woman would be hard enough. Creating a family of his own would be even harder.

"Even if I found a woman from our clan I could...accept, I wouldn't have children with her."

Athan rolled his eyes in exasperation. "That's what I'm suggesting, you idiot."

"And I won't be bed-hopping either, Athan. My scruples won't allow it, for one thing, and it would store up more trouble for the future. Mihail would never put up with it, and neither would most of our people. Kharova would be blown apart."

Athan nodded. "You're probably right. So marry someone from Mihail's side, then."

"No."

"Then you've painted yourself into a corner. Won't marry inside our clan, won't marry outside it. Won't have children with one of our women, won't have children with one of theirs. I can't find any escape clauses there, Leo." Athan was distracted for a second as a man appeared and whispered to him. Athan groaned. "Sorry, Leo. I've got to go. I forgot I was supposed to be meeting some foreign chair warmer ten minutes ago."

Leo sighed, trying not to smile. "I thought that was my job?"

"This isn't politics. It's someone from a logistics company, to talk about lines of supply. I was supposed to be getting him together with our guys, but I kind of ran out of time. Not enough hours in the day!"

This time Leo did grin. "You need a PA. You can have Krisia if you like."

Athan jumped. "Hell, no! Lord save me from bossy women. Anyway, she's too loyal to you."

"No, she's loyal to Kharova. If I could convince her she'd serve our country better by serving you, she'd be more than happy to oblige."

"Don't you dare!" Athan said, but his brother cut the connection with a flourish.

Leo brooded over the blank screen before picking up his phone. "Krisia? Come in here, please. I need your opinion on something."

She was at his side so fast Leo suspected she'd been hovering outside. "Take a seat. I want to ask you about something Sara suggested." He sighed when he saw her scowl.

"I hope you're not asking for my approval, Your—I mean, Leo."

"No, I'm not. But Sara thinks you're in love with me."

Krisia lost her breath as though she'd been punched in the stomach.

"If it's true, she doesn't want to do anything to hurt or upset you."

The change in Krisia's expression made him want to laugh. She was weighing her automatic dislike of Sara against news that the woman had a considerate side. "That's...very...thoughtful of her," she said, with every word sounding painful. "But why would she care about me?"

"She's been deceived in the past. She can't stand by and watch it happening to anyone else."

"You're saying she wants my approval, so she can have an affair with you?" It wasn't quite a snarl, but it came pretty close.

"Neither of us needs your approval about anything," Leo replied. "But we both have standards. It never occurred to me you might be in love with me. Sara made me realise I could have missed the signs. So I ask again: Are you in love with me?"

Krisia shifted inside her immaculate black suit. "I want what's best for our country. That means serving you."

"Hmm. As you didn't answer my actual question, I'll take that as a no. In which case, I've got a proposition for you."

Krisia looked still more uneasy. Leo laughed. "Relax, it's nothing terrible. Though it will mean even more work in the short term. I need you to become Athan's PA."

She tensed. "You can't mean that! My duty is here, with you!"

"No, you keep saying your duty is to help your country. You're an exceptional PA. Athan needs your skills more than I do. This morning he forgot about a meeting he'd organised. Luckily it wasn't anything serious, but next time it might be an ambassador who's left kicking his heels in an empty room. That can't be allowed to happen. Athan could use you, Krisia, although he won't admit it. You'll still be in charge of the arrangements for my coronation, but from now on you'll be working for Athan."

"You're trying to get rid of me, so you can spend more time with that woman!" She pouted.

Leo stood up, planting his hands on the desk with a bang. Krisia went pale and stepped back.

"I've told you before, her name is Sara. You'll call her that, or 'Miss Astley,' in my presence. You keep reminding me I'm king, and should behave like one. Well, a ruler expects total, unthinking obedience from his subjects, so maybe I'm not a natural king. I expect all my subjects to think for themselves, but if Kharovans want me on their throne, they must do as I say. And I say you'll serve our country better by working for Athan than by staying with me. Are you going to argue with your king?"

Leo was cold determination. The transformation into a total monarch made Krisia gulp. "No, Your Majesty," she whispered, backing away.

This time, Leo ignored the way she added his title. Sometimes, like it or not, he had to accept it. Picking up his jacket and phone, he followed her out of the door. "Don't worry. You'll love working for Athan," he assured her as he headed for the lift. He waited until its doors closed behind him before letting a satisfied smile spread across his face.

Chapter Nine

For the next few days Leo and Sara idled about, sailing Neroli around the coast and lazing in the sun. They talked about Leo's home, and the problems of his people. She loved the way his eyes lit up whenever he spoke about the improvements he would make to his business. He was determined to stop everyone living in the past, although he knew some would never accept change however hard he tried to persuade them. Sara used her professional tact to suggest ways to chauffeur-drive them into the present, rather than catapulting them straight into Leo's exciting vision of the future.

In turn, she got a whole new perspective on her own life. Using her skills to help Leo gave her a great sense of satisfaction. In a funny way, devising ideas with him was really relaxing. It took a while for her to realise she'd managed a complete about-face. She dreaded the idea of going back to work at ACS. The prospect hung over her like a threat.

Leo took her to Athens to lift her mood, but it didn't work. The thought of leaving the peace of Paradise was only part of the problem. Her biggest challenge would be saying good-bye to him. "I'm going to miss all this so much," she confided as they walked through the ancient city. She waited for him to ask if she would miss him too. His silence spoke volumes, and it wasn't what she wanted to hear. "Sometimes, I wish I'd never given in and come to Greece."

"Misery!" Leo teased. "I'm sure a stroll down Voukourestiou Street will revive you."

He was wrong. Nothing could fill the aching emptiness she felt whenever she thought about abandoning Leo to face his future alone, but she did her best to pretend. The displays of handmade jewelry set on glass in bone-white surroundings were a big distraction. Their cool elegance took her breath away. It was difficult to get it back again, when the next shop displayed a solitary designer dress draped with the perfect accessories of a toning silk scarf and understated purse.

"Does anything catch your eye?" Leo asked.

"All of it." Sara swung another look along the street of a thousand fantasies.

"But you haven't bothered to go inside any of the shops yet!"

"I don't want to disturb the staff if I don't intend to buy."

He nudged her playfully. "How will you know, if you don't try anything for size?"

"Everything must cost an absolute fortune, Leo. Nothing I've seen so far has had a price tag attached. That means trouble."

"Go ahead. Have what you like. I've got all my cards with me." He tapped the bulge of his wallet.

Sara was horrified. "No fear! Thanks, but I was brought up only to use credit when there's no alternative."

He pulled out his leather fold and flipped through it. "That's okay. I've got debit cards too, if it makes you feel better."

"No!" Sara brought her hand down on his, desperate to stop him embarrassing her. "Thank you, but no. Window shopping is my favourite fantasy. Once things go inside a bag, all the fun goes out of it for me."

"Don't you enjoy swinging carriers with designer names on them?"

"It all depends on what's inside."

A noisy scene in a side street interrupted them. An exasperated mother was wrestling her screaming toddler out of a buggy. With the child under one arm, she was trying to scrape a fallen globe of ice cream out of the stroller, and back into its wafer.

Sara was horrified. "She's never going to give that back to the baby, after it fell into the seat?"

Leo called to the woman, then disappeared up the side street and into a tiny shop. Sara guessed what he was doing, and went forward to lend a hand with mopping up the buggy. "Here—I've got some tissues in my bag." She held out a packet to the flushed and anxious woman.

Sara hoped to hear the Greek equivalent of thanks, I'll hold my baby while you swab out the seat. No such luck. The baby was dumped into her arms. Sara braced herself for another squall of screaming. The movement set her earrings dancing. That caught the baby's attention. It stopped crying, transfixed. She shook her head again to make the earrings bounce some more. As she looked up she caught the eye of a man in the distance. He was staring toward her, and talking into a phone. It was the same man who had dropped Krisia's book. Sara squinted against the glare of the sun, trying to get a clearer view of him, but a noisy gaggle of tourists straggled past, distracting her. Once they'd gone, the man was nowhere to be seen.

Leo came out of the shop, brandishing a prize and wearing the expression of a man who had everything under control. "One new ice cream."

Sara squeaked, and took a step back. She clutched the baby as though Leo was offering it a live snake.

"What's the matter?"

"Seriously, Leo? You'd give this little one chocolate, on a hot day like today? When he's dressed all in white?" She ran the fabric of the baby's angel top through her fingers. "And this feels like silk, too."

The look on Leo's face would have melted an iron doorstop. Her heart turned over as he muttered something under his breath, then said: "I didn't think. I just asked for the best they had."

She smiled. "It's very kind, but I think you'd better hand it straight over to Mom."

The baby was too entranced by Sara's earrings to have noticed the ice cream. Leo watched like an alien species. In contrast, Sara was beginning to enjoy herself. Holding the child wasn't as difficult and scary as she expected. It felt nice to be grinned at by somebody who didn't have an ulterior motive (or a full set of perfect white teeth) for a change.

She tried an experiment, and jiggled the baby in the way she'd seen people do it on TV. The child gurgled, then snatched her left earring. Sara tried not to howl with pain, but Leo was there in a flash, unwinding the chubby paw. When the baby locked on to Leo's finger instead, it was his turn to pull a face. "I'm not keen on this. It's sticky."

"That'll be the thin layer of ice cream. And this is a 'he' not an 'it!'" Sara hissed.

"Really? How can you tell?"

"It's obvious," she said, airily.

The grateful mother held out her hands for her baby and cooed her thanks on behalf of baby Calista.

Once the little girl was belted into her buggy, Leo handed the chocolate ice cream into her mother's protective custody.

He kept a straight face until they were out of the mother's earshot. Then he laughed. "Obvious, was it? I've never heard of a boy called Calista before!"

Sara flushed. The smell of baby powder was still fresh on her skin, and it was having a strange effect. She'd never been one for babies before. Now she was wondering why not. That uncertainty made her feel uncomfortable, and she snapped. "I'm a businesswoman, not a nursery maid."

"Although I'd say you were handling the work wonderfully then, right up until the point when you called that woman's daughter a son."

"I am very good at my job!" she told him through gritted teeth.

He stopped laughing. "Of course you are. I can see that. You're calm and capable in a crisis, with a cheerful disregard for any little inconsistencies in your argument. I'm sure you'll make someone a wonderful husband."

She refused to let him make fun of her. "I can take care of myself. You're the one who ought to look out, Leo Gregoryan. It's one thing to be at home in the mountains or on the sea, but any child of yours will need to be looked after by someone who knows what they're doing." She tutted. "To think—giving chocolate to a baby dressed in white!"

"You're beginning to sound like Krisia."

That was a low blow. "Where is your PA these days, anyway?"

Leo turned the loose change over in his pockets. Sara knew what that meant. "So you two have fallen out?"

"I don't need a PA in attendance while I'm on holiday."

"I thought she was on holiday too?"

"Krisia is welded to her job. So am I. Let's just say we had a professional difference of opinion," Leo said in a diplomatic tone of voice, "so I've learned from the callous way ACS treated you. Rather than disappoint her, I've promoted her out of my life."

"Congratulations to Krisia!" Sara said, with real feeling. "But I thought you were at the top of your family heap? How much higher could she go?"

"That's why we fell out." Leo took his hands out of his pockets and strolled on. "Krisia's serious, studious, and steady. She's everything my brother isn't. But she loves a challenge, so I've given her to Athan, as his PA. They'll both go far. If they can avoid killing each other in the process."

"So where does this leave you? Without a PA, but with potential trouble at home?"

Leo kicked a pebble out of his way. "There's always trouble at home. But Athan's the one to sort it out. And as for my PA...her perfect replacement is standing right in front of me. You and I have got on well together over the past few days, Sara. I want you to be Krisia's stand-in while you're here."

Sara's heart sank. She knew what Leo thought about mixing business with pleasure, although her own boundaries were getting blurry. She wanted a safe, pain-free life. Hanging out with Leo was a wonderful distraction, but that wouldn't last. Taking him up on his offer would mean she could work beside him, but that would be all there was to their relationship. Work. The idea of a holiday romance with him was tempting her more and more, but she had never been interested in one-night stands. If there was no future for them, why risk the pain of having to part?

Trying to hide her confusion, she laughed. "If there's anything I can do to help you while I'm here, fine. But I'm more concerned about what happens when you get back home to find a mountain of paperwork, and with no PA."

"You don't need to worry about that. When I'm not on holiday, I have more people fawning around me than I can handle. In fact in the words of Abraham Lincoln, there are too many pigs for the—" He stopped, and looked uncomfortable.

"What?"

"No. There are limits to what a man can say in front of a woman, even if that woman is you, Sara."

That puzzled her. "I don't know whether to be offended or flattered."

"When you're so allergic to compliments, it hardly matters, does it? Never mind. We're here to enjoy ourselves, not bicker over details."

When they returned to Paradise Island, they strolled through the village rather than go straight back to the hotel. To escape the sunshine they dodged into the shade between the sparkling white houses. The heat wasn't so easy to avoid. Taking a sharp left turn past a small tower that looked like the decoration from a giant wedding cake, they followed a warren of lanes that opened into a tiny courtyard. It was complete with a burbling fountain, and a little old lady bundled up from head to foot in black. Her gnarled fingers were working a spider web of fine white lace. She smiled at them, and said a few words in Greek. Leo chatted to her, while they admired her work. Sara couldn't understand what he was saying, but she knew it wasn't the same language she'd heard him use with Krisia. "It never occurred to me people could still live like this," she said.

A familiar sound echoed through the little courtyard. The old lady dipped her head in apology, reached into the pocket of her skirt and drew out a phone. Sara and Leo wandered away to give her some privacy. "Well, who'd have thought someone like that would have a mobile?" Sara said. "Although I suppose it's the obvious answer to looking after elderly relatives. They can call her up to make sure she's okay. It must be easy for old people to overdo things in this heat."

"There you go—jumping to conclusions again. I can tell you don't speak Greek."

"I suspect it's why my PA was so pleased I agreed to come here at last," Sara laughed. "I can't ask for directions to the nearest cyber café."

"That woman is talking to her accountant about a series of lacemaking lectures she's been giving. She told me she was expecting his call."

Sara gave him a poke. "You're making it up!"

"Maybe, maybe not. You have to admit it sounds less condescending than your version," he teased, catching at her hand.

She nodded. "You're right. I shouldn't have assumed anything. My working life is so well researched, I never normally do that." She looked embarrassed. "This holiday's making me impetuous."

Leo stopped. When she did the same and turned to face him, he put his hand up to her face. With the ball of his thumb he gently smoothed out the crease between her brows. "That's no bad thing. You were sent here to rest and relax. Don't let your prejudices get in the way of that."

Sara closed her eyes, trying to tell herself it was a reflex action at the movement of his hand so close to her face. The feel of his skin against hers had nothing to do with it. The woodland notes of his cologne were a far more powerful temptation. "Especially when I do things like this," he said, and kissed her.

It was what Sara had wanted it all along. She'd managed to deflect him often enough to think she was safe from temptation. When he held her and savored her kisses like vintage champagne, she knew she'd been wrong to resist. He filled her mind and tantalized her body until she could think of nothing else. When their lips parted, she rested her head against his chest, closed her eyes and tried to catch her breath. "That shouldn't have happened," he said, although his arms were still wound tight around her body, holding her close.

Sara's eyes flew open. "I'm the one who's supposed to say things like that."

"I've saved you the effort," he said, without letting her go. "In the same way I'm never going to give you the chance to offend my sense of honor again. Let me take you out to dinner this evening."

Sara pulled away from him. His kiss was so intoxicating she knew dinner wouldn't be the main thing on his menu. Or hers. "No. One thing will lead to another, and I'm supposed to be relaxing, not setting myself up for another personal drama. You shouldn't distract me like this."

"It's called helping you to unwind, and make the most of your stay here. And speaking of which, I'm living on borrowed time, don't forget," he said with a roguish twinkle.

"That," she said, "Is nothing short of emotional blackmail, Mr. Gregoryan."

"I know."

Sara pressed her lips together and tried to disapprove. She couldn't. Her whole body ached to take a risk with Leo. "Meeting a man who's open about his motives is so unusual, I'm tempted to give you a try, Mr. Gregoryan."

"Does this mean I've lost my air of mystery?" He squeezed her playfully.

"It means I'll agree to a short trial." Sara said—but she didn't tell him it was her willpower she would be putting to the test.

As she dressed for her night out with Leo, Sara wondered if she could persuade him to open up about his unwanted career change. He'd worked such miracles on her; he would have made a brilliant doctor.

He's pretty well qualified in a lot of other areas, too, she thought, strolling barefoot through the dressing room of her suite. It was lovely to take her time getting ready for once. In London, her life—her working life— moved at ninety miles an hour. There was no time left for socializing outside of work. She was always at the office.

This short break had shown her a whole new way of life. She hadn't realized how much pleasure there could be in dawdling. At first, she'd resented being pushed off the daily treadmill. Now she was learning all over again the simple pleasure of taking her time. She could idle over selecting her outfit, instead of grabbing the first thing to hand.

After a long deliberation, she chose silk underwear in pale peach, edged with cream lace. As usual, it was a decision she made to please herself, and no one else. She twirled in front of a full-length mirror, loving the sensation of fine fabric moving over her skin. It made her feel good, and she smiled at her reflection. Standing in a patch of sunlight dressed in silk underwear and high heels, she tried to decide between a full-length dress in green satin, or a little cocktail-length number in blue moiré. This was the kind of heaven she had never experienced before. She reveled in the sensation as time slipped away. With minutes to go before Leo was supposed to be calling for her, she decided on the body-skimming emerald dress with its shimmer of gold threads. It complemented her mane of auburn hair, and shimmered in the low rays of the sun. A dusting of blusher and a quick slick of lipstick, and she checked the mirror again. Then she nodded. Leo was worth dressing up for—but then, so was she.

She was fastening a pair of gold droplets into her ears when there was a knock at the door.

"It's me. Leo."

"I'm impressed. You're right on time." She crossed the room.

"Naturally," he called through the door. "To be

early is needy. To be late is unforgivable."

She opened the door, and enjoyed seeing him startle.

"You're ready too?"

"Of course. I agree with you. You said you'd be here at eight, so I got ready in the faint hope you'd be as good as your word. It turns out you're the first man I've met who not only owned a watch, but knew how to use it."

"You sound surprised."

"I am—and you look it!"

He ran an appreciative gaze over her sleek green dress. It concealed more than it revealed, but its cut slicked across her hips to show off her figure. "You look good."

Sara feigned disappointment. "Is that it? I was aiming for a breathless 'wow!'"

"Then actions should speak louder than words." He scooped her into his arms for a kiss. Moving fast, Sara put her hands against his chest and resisted.

"That's what I'm afraid of."

He released her slowly, and with regret. "You're right. I can't deny everyone at The Philomela the chance to see you looking like this."

"Wow...I mean, so that's where we're going? I've heard their chef is hoping for a second Michelin star. Thank goodness I made a bit of an effort," she said, to prove she hadn't done it just for him.

"You'll make that chef see a few stars while he's waiting. It makes me glad I've put on my second-best suit."

Sara hadn't expected him to play her at her own game. He was wearing an immaculate tuxedo, complete with crisp white shirt and black velvet bow tie, and looked perfect. That didn't stop her rising to his bait. "Are you saying an evening out with me only deserves second best?"

Leo gave her the smile of a man making fine distinctions. "Our unplanned swim together made sure my best one is unwearable. My tailor is hard at work on the replacement. While he's a genius, he's not a miracle worker."

"Of course." Grabbing her bag and key card, Sara swung out of the suite and headed for the lift.

"What happened to your pedometer?"

"You noticed I'm not wearing it?"

"Call it professional interest."

"I was beginning to take my exercising a bit too seriously. If I couldn't make my twelve thousand steps per day because you and I had been lazing on the deck of Neroli, I got so stressed it was worse than doing no exercise at all. So I binned it."

"Swimming and taking it easy are a better bet when you're supposed to be on holiday. It's all I do," Leo said.

And you're looking pretty good on it, she thought. "Then I'm very happy to take that sort of medical advice."

He gestured her into the elevator.

A valet was parking Leo's car in front of the hotel as they stepped outside.

"What's it like to drive one of these?" Sara asked as he opened the passenger door for her.

"Try it."

She recoiled. "No. No, I can't..."

"Sara? What's up? I've never offered anyone else

the chance before, but I'm pretty sure that's an unusual reaction."

"I had a bad accident, and I haven't driven since," she said, diving into the car and pulling the door out of his hands to slam it shut. Revealing her lapse to Leo made her feel terrible. As he walked round the back of the car, her mind went into overdrive. He was bound to tease her about this so she braced herself, ready to laugh it all off.

He opened the door, and got in. Sara held her breath. He started the car and sent it down the myrtle-lined drive like an arrow. "Aren't you going to tell me not to be so stupid?" she asked, when he said nothing.

"No. Because I understand," he replied.

They turned out onto the coast road. To one side, the land fell away into the sea. While Sara gazed out at the spectacular scenery and foaming breakers, Leo maintained a tense silence. In his experience of women, she was unique. In a matter of days, she had caused him to think about his future in a completely different way. He had spent a long time that day in another call to his brother, discussing their next move. Athan was unconvinced about Leo's latest idea, but he promised to get things moving at home.

All Leo had to do now was broach the subject with Sara. Knowing it could be the conversation that shattered their tentative new friendship, he dropped a first pebble into their companionable silence. "As you pulled out early from the last dinner we had together, I calculate my charity consultation account with you is still in credit, Sara."

"I didn't realise all this was still on a professional basis?"

"There's no need to look so disappointed!" I could leave it at that, Leo thought. We could have a perfect evening, and I'd keep her friendship. That's all I want. And besides, if anything goes wrong, or if Athan can't manage his part in my miracle, I'd lose everything.

He saw her try to hide a squirm of distaste, and swallow before she could manage to go on. "Neither of us is looking forward to going back to our respective jobs, but if they need to be done then I'm a realist, Leo. Work is work, and bills need paying."

"I know."

She didn't react to his comforting tone in the way he expected. Slumping back in her seat, she turned a look of disbelief on him. "How can a great, caring, intelligent guy like you abandon a career you were born to follow, to take up a position you don't want?"

Leo took heart from her flattery, and smiled. "My relative Mihail wants to try his luck with a…takeover bid. That would be disastrous for all concerned. Especially my brother."

"Now who's letting their prejudices show?" He felt her scrutiny sharpen. Then she hitched a breath and said, "And you called me paranoid!"

He didn't answer, but flicked on the car's indicator with more force than he intended. As he parked at the restaurant, she twisted in her seat and put her hand on his arm to stop him getting out. "May I make a suggestion?"

"Can I stop you?"

"Nothing is worth all the trauma you're putting yourself through. Not even family loyalty—and believe me, I'd kill to be part of something that inspires feelings like yours. Your talent is for caring. Your need to do that is more important than being head of some tin-pot organization."

Leo moved under her gentle hand. How many sleepless hours had he spent thinking the same thing in the years since his older brother Zacari fell ill? "But I will always be the king," he said in an unguarded flash.

She waved his words away. "No job title means anything if you can't be true to yourself, Leo!"

That shocked him. Was it so obvious? He had to change the subject. "We've got time to check out the bar before dinner. I need to ask you something, and you're going to need a drink first."

"In view of all the calories I'm hoping to take in tonight, it had better be something non—alcoholic. I'll stick to mineral water, please," she said.

"Then brace yourself. It's going to be an exciting evening." Pulling away from her hand, he got out of the car.

Chapter Ten

The restaurant was in a converted stable block, built around a cobbled courtyard. Wisteria and ivy rambled over a pergola. Among the greenery, candles held in glass globes gave out a soft glow. Leo escorted Sara into the building, ducking to avoid the low lintel.

"Are you sure you wouldn't like something more exotic?"

She had been taking in every detail of the bar. Baskets of large ripe citrus fruit flanked a sophisticated juicer, like the one leased by Apis Concierge Solutions. "Go on, then. I'll have a fresh St. Clement's on ice, please. It'll ease me back into my work routine."

"We're here to help you forget all that. Remember?" Leo ordered the same for himself.

"It's tricky. For years ACS has been the first thing I think about when I wake up, and the last thing that's on my mind at night. Look where it's got me."

"I suspect they've done you a favor." He ignored her scowl and went on, "You say this new board member is a smooth talker. You're a proven success on the ground. So let him talk at the executive level, while you deal with the practical side. You'll complement each other."

Sara ran her fingers over a slight dent in her cheek. "History suggests otherwise. That's why I started spending even more time at work, and away from home."

"People who do that are usually compensating for a hellish private life."

"I don't have to do it any more. As I've said before, if I make a mistake, I learn from it and move on."

"That's why I want you to complete my consultation while we're here," Leo said.

Picking up their drinks himself rather than leaving them to be delivered by a waiter, he ambled outside to a secluded terrace at the back of the restaurant. Although it had a stunning view of a peaceful wooded valley, it was deserted. Sara walked to the low rail surrounding the paved area. Leo watched her from a distance, waiting for the perfect moment to speak.

He wanted her, but she couldn't be allowed to want him. Sara was his perfect woman in every way but one. She wasn't the Kharovan princess his culture demanded he should marry.

Leo had devised a compromise. Now he had to try it out on Sara. He'd run through all the options in his mind, but as Athan said, each was as mad and unworkable as the rest. Whatever happened, Leo was bound to lose Sara, the carefree woman he had spent so long unwinding. Once she understood his destiny, nothing would ever be the same again. If she didn't walk out on him straight away, he would have to send her packing. It was the only way to save her.

I should have explained right at the start, but couldn't imagine how. No relationship can survive a revelation like this. I've left it too long.

The silence was so deep, Sara heard Leo exhale. She wandered farther away from him, expecting him to shadow her. When he didn't, she stopped to admire a terracotta planter of beautiful cream lilies. "Have you brought me out here because you didn't want to be overheard?"

"Yes," he said, but took his time in joining her. "I've been impressed from the start by all your many...assets, Sara."

She waited for him to smile. When he didn't, she glanced around. They were still alone on the terrace. Shapes moved around inside the restaurant, silhouetted in the windows, but no one in there was taking any notice of what might be going on out here. She sipped her drink. Leo was standing so close to her she could bask in his warmth. She thought back over the times they had shared over the past few days, and the all-too-brief occasion when he held her. Feeling the steady beat of his pulse against her body was an experience she wanted to relive, over and over again. She'd considered making the initial move, but inviting him to dinner on that first evening hadn't met with his approval. Their kiss in Athens had been a delicious start, but so far Leo showed no sign of taking things any further. "Yes. I noticed," she said.

He was holding his glass by the rim. As he swirled the contents around, he seemed to be paying more attention to his drink than to her. "I haven't been entirely straight with you."

She made a sinuous movement, drawing herself up to her full height.

"One of the many reasons I don't want to take up my new position is that I'll be expected to marry a suitable relative. And the sooner the better," he went on.

Sara was an old hand at absorbing blows, but this one almost caught her out. She hadn't been prepared for such a brutal end to their friendship. It took her a while to starch her expression into a brittle smile. "A doctor paddling in the shallow end of the gene pool? It's no wonder you didn't want the job."

He put his hand to his brow, then dragged it down over his face. "Yes. And it's even worse than you think. My family shares a genetic condition that makes marrying even a distant relative inadvisable. But you may hold the solution to all my problems, Sara. You're a dedicated hard worker who hasn't been getting the recognition she deserves. You're disillusioned with your current employers, so I want you to come and work for me on a special project. It calls for an extraordinary woman. I'll never find a better candidate than you."

His chest rose as he took a deep breath. Then he took another one. "I'll go home and marry the woman selected for me, but it'll be a legal contract and nothing more. Nothing...physical. Then, after a suitable interval, you'll find me the perfect surrogate mother for my children."

Sara's mouth fell open with a mixture of shock and horror. She tried to find her voice. Agreeing to stand in for his PA was one thing, but this was ridiculous. All she could do was gesture, first at him, then at the heavens, in complete exasperation.

"I don't need to remind you, this is a matter of the utmost confidentiality."

When she found her voice, it was high and unsteady. "You are joking?"

"Not at all. It's a compromise. My wife will be my

social and political ally, while my children will be genetically healthy and raised by their natural mother."

"That's big of you!" she said with the shock of sarcasm. He rocked on his heels.

"She would be acknowledged as their nanny, of course. There could be no suggestion of her true role, beyond the nursery door. It's not perfect, but it means I'd have a popular wife who's prepared for that role, and healthy children as well. What matters to me is that they will be raised in a family setting, well away from the dangers of Kharovan life."

"Kharova!" she exclaimed. "That place? I might have guessed. ACS almost lost a contract with them because of their prehistoric ideas. If you come from there, it's no wonder you've dreamed up such a mad, Neanderthal notion!"

"I'm offering you the job of matchmaker because you're the perfect woman for the job," he continued with dogged patience. "And I like you, Sara. No, it's more than that. I admire you."

"Well, you've got a pretty funny way of showing it! So that's what all this is about." Her voice was cold. "The trips on your yacht, the sightseeing? The treats? All the time, you were softening me up so I'd run Operation Rent-a-Womb for you!"

"No! Not at all. I asked you to share all those things because I thought you'd enjoy them. As we spent time together, I became more and more sure of you. This scheme felt like a stroke of genius when I discussed it with Athan, but I respect your judgment. You hate the idea. Fine. I get it. Forget I ever said anything. Let's move on."

"No, Leo! No, I don't think you do get it!" Sara

blazed. "Can't you see what you've done? You mentioned all this as casually as you invited me out to dinner! What sort of a man are you? Good grief—the sheer arrogant nerve! Just so your business carries on in a perfect, unbroken line! I thought you were the nicest guy I'd ever met, and all the time you were leading up to this!"

"That's not true," he said, which didn't make her feel any better.

"I'm amazed you feel the need to get married at all, Leo, with all your go-ahead twenty-first-century ideas! Why not have yourself cloned instead? Yes—that's a good idea," she mocked, getting into her stride. "Shed a few cells, and once you've given them to someone else to worry about, you can get on with your life without a care in the world until Leo Gregoryan Mark Two is ready to take on the weight of responsibility. Imagine it! An endless procession of male heirs, all perfect copies of you, produced for no better reason than to shoulder your family's burden down through history!" she raged.

"Okay—I said forget it!" he butted in as she paused to snatch a breath. "Trust you to bring an attitude like that to a professional consultation."

That brought her up short. "Are you saying I'm bad tempered?"

"I couldn't possibly comment."

Her nostrils flared. "I'll have you know, I haven't got where I am today by not being able to fight my own corner, Leo Gregoryan."

He took a measured sip of his drink. "I don't doubt that."

Sara was as tense as a bowstring, and breathing

hard. She had to prove she could keep a grip on her anger.

"While you're so busy 'fighting your corner,' don't forget other people have feelings too. I know it's a crazy idea. I've known it from the start, but I've run out of alternatives. That's why I asked for your advice, not your judgment."

Her lashes flickered. She could see it had taken him a lot to confide in her. Taking a few steadying breaths, she unclenched her fists. "I suppose you're saying it's a fine line between being assertive, and being a bully, Leo. I know, I know. I'm sorry"—she dashed a hand across her face in frustration—"but my father—whoever he was—shared your casual attitude to parenting. I can't forget what a struggle my mom had when he left us in the lurch. That's not happening to me, or anyone else if I can help it."

"I lost my own mother because my father made the wrong choice of wife."

There was such feeling in his voice that Sara managed to push her anger aside. "So you decided to hedge your bets," she said into the quiet of the evening.

Leo made the sort of noise in the back of his throat that could have meant anything. Coming so close to the arrival of a waiter to invite them in to their table, he must have calculated it would put anyone off his trail. Anyone except Sara. "Okay. I get it," she said.

He's got a past with women, and it affecting his view of the future. That explains a lot, Sara thought. *He wants the respectability of marriage without the pain of a real relationship. That's why he's no keener on getting close to somebody than I am.*

She wondered why this didn't feel like a good

thing. It probably had a lot to do with Leo's smile. She could take any amount of a smile like that, whatever mad ideas he came out with.

The air-conditioning was working almost too well as Leo escorted her to their table. As the waiter pulled out a chair for her, she gave a little shiver. Without a word, Leo had them moved to a table in an alcove where they were shielded from draughts as well as onlookers.

"I'm reconsidering my whole attitude to you," she said as they chose what to order.

He lowered his menu. His face was serious, and his dark eyes held her gaze with intent.

"I think we're too alike, Leo. I'd love to help you, because I can see you're in a fix. I love challenges and—well, I love your company. That's a big admission for me to make, believe me. I wouldn't have told you if you hadn't come up with that crackpot suggestion. It made me wonder if you're any different from men who see me as nothing more than a means to an end."

The waiter came to take their order. Half expecting Leo to play his part of man from a country where women did as they are told, Sara was flustered when he asked what she would like. On impulse, she ordered poached chicken with morels. Leo opted for the same, but he was more interested in her.

The moment the waiter left, Leo leaned forward to murmur a question so no one else would hear. "Is your knowledge of men so extensive you can tar us all with the same brush?"

Sara refused to raise her eyes to meet his. "You aren't going to goad me into answering that."

He was silent and still for so long, she couldn't stand it. Raising her head as the waiter delivered their appetizers she braced herself to withstand his expression. She expected it to be smug with an air of we'll see about that. Instead, he was investigating his tiny glass of iced soup. His face was a grim mask.

"What's the matter?"

"Nothing."

He had to be lying. Sara put down her spoon. At the clink of silver against bone china, he looked up.

"Is there something wrong with your smoothie?" she prodded.

"No."

"Then what is it? You've gone from being the man about town who rescues women, buys ice cream for children, and asks me to find him a surrogate for his child, to someone who acts like cold pea soup is the most absorbing thing on the planet. I can't have scuppered all your plans so easily. There's something else going on. What is it? Spill."

Leo finished his appetizer, then aligned his spoon beside its empty glass before replying. "If this is the way you carry on over dinner, it's no wonder men have trouble with you."

"They don't. I have trouble with them."

"That's a matter of opinion. I'm beginning to think it's not so much a case of men not understanding you— I'm sure they understand you too well, Sara. You'd be an unbeatable threat to anyone who wanted to play the mediaeval despot. Alexander the Great? *Phht!* You could have driven off Genghis Khan and all his hordes."

She compressed her face in a frown. A few days

ago she would have been delighted to hear anyone say that about her. Now, she wasn't so sure. She respected Leo, and liked him. For him of all people to describe her like that was a big wake-up call. She never appreciated those.

Picking up her spoon again, she started on her own appetizer.

"I recognize the signs, Sara. It's how my older brother Zacari felt about me. He always wanted me to do things his way."

"It's a shame your brother's not here now. He and I could have swapped notes."

"Yes. You don't know how much of a shame it is," Leo said with feeling.

"It sounds like Zacari has made a better job of escaping from your family firm than you have."

A nerve pulsed in his jaw. "You could say that. He died."

Sara froze. The spoon fell from her fingers. "Leo! Oh, I'm so sorry. What an idiot I am, blundering on..."

He threw down his napkin, reached across the table and grabbed her fluttering hands. "Stop. You weren't to know."

"That doesn't excuse me sounding off."

"Of course it does." He clasped his large warm hands over her slender fingers.

"So that's what happened. Zacari died, and you gave up your own career to take his place."

"Yes. I was torn. I still am, to be honest. If I'd stayed in medicine then maybe I could have gone into research to help find a cure for the cancer that killed him."

Sara smiled. "I'm not so sure that would have been

a good idea. You would still have been devoting your life to doing something that wasn't part of your plan. The choice you made then was the right one for you at the time."

Leo squeezed her hands, releasing them as their main course was brought to the table. "I had dreams of discovering things down a microscope, but I love the people part of medicine more," he went on as they began their meal. "You're right. I wasn't cut out to be a back-room boy."

"No, I can't see you presiding over a board meeting when you could be playing the fool in a children's ward," Sara smiled, which widened into laughter when he responded.

"Are you suggesting I'm still a child at heart?"

"Not when it comes to women, you aren't. At least, that isn't how it felt when you were examining my leg."

He grinned at her, his eyes alive with mischief again. His expression sent warm fronds of desire coiling deep within her body. She moved in her seat, and beneath the table her leg connected with his. Her natural impulse would have been to leap away as though scalded, if it had been anyone but Leo. He made her want to linger. When he didn't move, she rolled her heel so the inside of her calf brushed against the fine cloth of his suit. He smiled, slow and sweet.

"That was different. You weren't sick, you were injured. And within seconds of meeting you, Sara Astley, I decided you were more than capable of looking after yourself."

"That's what you thought?" She gave a derisive laugh, and let her instep come to rest against his ankle. "Then give me an Oscar. It was all an act."

"That's more common than you think," Leo said, dissecting his chicken.

She went straight onto the defensive. "I suppose that means you do the same?"

"Not me, no. But I know someone who does," he said in a voice low with disapproval. "I like to keep things light and clear. Then there can be no misunderstandings."

"And then there's your rule about not fooling around with your work colleagues."

He finished his meal and put down his knife and fork. Then he planted his elbows on the table and watched her over his netted fingers. "That helps. And my existing team know the hazards of my life too well to want to get involved with me on a personal level."

"Does that mean you've got a lot of dangerous hobbies, like tombstoning or motocross?" Sara asked, trying not to make it sound like a loaded question.

"Hobbies? No, I don't have time for them. And I'll bet you don't, either. Your head is too full of work. There can't be much room for anything else."

"I hope that's a backhanded compliment. Otherwise I'll be asking what happened to your admiration for my business sense."

"That's taken as read. You're a clever woman."

"And you are a very plausible man," she countered, and felt him move below the table so the contact between them increased.

"True, although I don't exploit the fact. I've always selected my partners with care. I do the asking, always tell the truth, and make it clear when it's over. When I choose a woman I aim to please, and hit the target. Every time."

"Except when you misfire, and ask an innocent woman to forget her principles and treat babies as a business venture."

Leo sat up, drew his feet back under his chair, and called for the dessert menu. It was difficult to hide his irritation. Asking Sara seemed like a good idea at the time. She had everything to recommend her as the perfect facilitator: fierce intelligence, together with drive, efficiency, and single-mindedness. She also had stubborn pride and a sharp tongue.

Once they selected their final course, he bent toward her and hissed his disapproval. "Leave it. I've admitted that asking you was an error of judgment. I'm never going there again. Believe me."

"Good," she said.

Leo was glad her reply was so forceful. It dampened down the simmering desire she provoked in him, but couldn't stifle it altogether. Instead, she became all the more desirable now she'd announced she was out of his reach. Over dessert and coffee he tried to bring her back within range, but it was difficult.

"With me, what you see is what you get," she said. "My life outside the office withered, until work became my whole existence. It's taken this enforced break to make me see what a mistake I made. Everyone was right—yes, you included. From now on I'm going to get my life back in balance and take a look at the view as I travel along. And nobody is going to drive their way through my money faster than I can earn it," she finished with an air of satisfaction. She drifted into reflective silence, but jumped back to life as the waiter arrived with their bill.

"Let me get this, Leo, since you paid for our dinner

at the hotel."

He flipped open his wallet and handed a card to the waiter.

"There's your answer, Sara."

As they headed out to the car, she felt like opening up. "Going home after this holiday to a house cluttered with cross-trainers but without anyone to talk to won't seem quite so bad now."

"Set the keep-fit stuff up in front of a TV. Then you can give your pedometer a workout, and let your mind freewheel at the same time."

His laughter was infectious. "Are you prescribing me homework, nearly-a-doctor Gregoryan?"

"Yes, I suppose I am."

"Then let's get back to the hotel, and hit the remote."

"Your place, or mine?" His voice was light and teasing, but Sara was struck by how far they had come in the space of a few hours. This was a man who had started their date by asking her to find a mother for his baby as if it was just another job. Now they were joking together. She didn't want this to slip into reverse, but were they friends, or was Leo the seasoned seducer trying a new tactic on her? She wasn't sure.

Trying to gain some thinking time, she gestured at the car keys in his hand. "Were you serious about letting me drive your car?"

"Be my guest."

He made sure she was settled in the driver's seat, before getting into the passenger side. That was a nice touch, but it made Sara nervous. His sports car was the most powerful vehicle she had ever driven. It was the last thing she would have chosen as her re-introduction to the road, but she was determined to conquer her fear. The car had never been driven so carefully before. The sheer drop below the coast road was a powerful incentive to keep her eyes on the road, and her wits about her. As they rounded the bay, a huge moon was rising out of the water.

"Look at that!" Sara gasped. "You could almost touch it!"

On impulse, she swung the car into the next viewpoint and parked nose-in to the panorama. She waited for Leo to hit imaginary brakes as his car prowled toward the cliff edge. He didn't, but he couldn't avoid snatching at the handbrake. In doing so he accidentally caught her dress too. Sara gave a little gasp, as she felt his hand linger. Was he waiting to see which way she would jump?

For long seconds, neither of them moved. Then she had to speak. "Why don't we get out and take a walk? It's such a beautiful night."

"Of course." His palm rested on the handbrake. The back of his hand was still touching the whisper-thin fabric that clung to her like a second skin. When she didn't move, he lifted his arm in a sweeping gesture that happened to draw his fingers along the length of her thigh. The hesitation in her breathing must have been unmistakable, but he got out of the car and went around to open the door for her.

He offered to help her out. "I can manage," she said.

"Old habits die hard, I'm afraid. Anyway, your leg is still healing."

"I'm not an invalid."

"Oh, I can see that."

Sara unfolded herself from the car and stood in the moonlight, enjoying the freedom. The crash of foaming breakers on one side and the chuckle of cicadas on the rocky hillside above them made London seem dull in comparison, and very far away. "I must have been mad to spend so much time in the office." She sighed.

"Marriage to your work is an arid, loveless relationship."

"I can see that now. Not that I'm after any other sort of relationship at the moment, though. I've done with all that for the time being. They aren't my thing."

"On the contrary, I think they're very much your thing. That's why you've been hurt in the past."

Sara didn't want to answer, but she needed to derail his train of thought. "Sometimes it's good to drop the shallow kissy-kissy client thing, and enjoy some meaningful time with another human being."

"It's something men do a lot, in particular. I've been guilty of skimming, myself," Leo said. "In my experience sex is a great answer to any problem. Let your body feel. If it's having a good time, then your whole life looks up. Everything seems better. Sex is supposed to be uncomplicated fun. It's when one person or the other gets busy with ties and jealousy and contracts, the trouble starts. But if your mind's unwinding, why not give your body a holiday too? Relax. Take my advice and forget all your expectations of a happy ever after. Do something wild for once. Who's to know? Let your body take the initiative, Sara. Take a chance. I can guarantee you won't regret it." His voice was quiet in the night.

She flinched.

"What's the matter?"

"Nothing."

A small dark shape flittered past.

"It's only a bat."

"Yes, that must have been it."

As if sensing her uncertainty, Leo took the initiative and caught hold of her hand.

Chapter Eleven

"Sara..." He breathed, sliding his arms around her.

She responded by lifting her hands and digging her fingers through his hair.

"Leo..." she moaned before he silenced her with a kiss.

Her body was so lissom he wanted to wind every inch of it around himself.

"Take me here, Leo. Now. Fast and hard."

The sudden change in her took him by surprise, and made him wary. "There's an emperor-sized bed and champagne on ice waiting back in my suite."

"But I want you now, Leo. Not in twenty minutes' time!"

This wasn't right. He wanted her to slow down. Covering her throat with kisses half muffled his voice. "Anticipation...the ultimate aphrodisiac..."

"Not for me, it isn't." She twisted out of his grasp. "I thought you wanted sex with no complications. So what are you waiting for? I don't want it to mean anything more to me than it does to you."

He stopped, shocked. "Sara? You can't be serious."

"I never joke about things like this."

He held her at arm's length. "No. You don't want this to be over as soon as possible, any more than I do. I refuse to make it a surgical procedure, performed without anaesthetic."

"It's more a rite of passage. I need to do it, to prove I can. Like getting back on a horse after a fall."

He was dumbfounded. "You mean you aren't looking forward to this?"

"I'm looking forward to having you, of course I am," she whispered, twining her arms around his neck. "But I know I won't be anything more than another notch on your bedpost, Leo. As long as I keep my mind fixed on that fact, I'll be fine."

He took her hands from his neck and held them. "Sara! Do you think so little of yourself you'd treat this as some sort of bizarre endurance test?"

"If I have no illusions, I won't be hurt or disappointed."

With a noise of disgust, he released her. "That's not how I look at it. And you know what? I'm not going to be a party to you wrecking your life. Let's get back to the hotel."

He stormed to his car and flung open the passenger door. As he did it, he knew the action had a violence the scene didn't need.

It'll serve me right if she burst into tears now, he thought.

Sara was silhouetted in the moonlight. He couldn't tell whether her outline was shimmering with hysteria, or if it was a trick of the light caused by staring at her too hard.

A sleepless gull racketed away seaward. A motorbike roared past, tearing a strip through the silence. It left ragged gaps allowing laughter to seep up from a beach bar, half a mile away.

The only thing Leo didn't hear was the sound of crying.

He had to break the impasse somehow. "Sara...you'll get cold standing there."

For half a dozen heartbeats, she never moved.

She must have heard me. She's playing deaf.

Then in her own good time she stalked the twenty yards to his car—and stepped into the driver's seat.

Icily indifferent to everything, she drove back to the Paradise Hotel. As she parked, Leo kept his hands well away from any contact with her thigh. He needn't have bothered. She had the driver's door open the moment the vehicle came to a standstill. She jumped out and disappeared into the foyer of the hotel, leaving his keys jangling in the ignition.

"So much for letting me hold the door open for you, my lady," Leo said, slamming the car shut with enough force to rattle all the glass in the hotel's lobby. The shock brought him to his senses. Rolling his head back on his shoulders, he wondered how he might have talked her round. That was when he saw a man looking at him from an upper window.

"Sorry about the disturbance," Leo added a mime to his apology to make the meaning clear. He flicked his car keys at the valet, and headed into the building.

Sara blundered through the reception area with her head down. She didn't stop until she was inside her suite with the door locked. Trembling from head to foot, she put a hand over her eyes. She had wrecked their evening. and all because it felt perfect. Given the chance to take pleasure to another level with a sultry night of passion, she'd pulled back. A switch flicked inside her brain. Leo's charm gave him access to her heart and soul until it was impossible to dislodge him, but instead of making her happy her instincts veered to the other extreme. She was afraid gorgeous Leo would turn into a monster once they got between the sheets. She'd seen it happen to a man before. Trying to scare Leo off by coming on too strong was her way of shifting the blame in case things went wrong.

He was the perfect escort, and that was how she wanted him to stay. It meant finishing the evening before sex started. Giving Leo that ultimatum—then and there or never—wrecked the moment, as she'd known it would. Deep down, she was terrified giving in to her need for him would wreck their friendship. Would all the respect and attraction she felt for him, and he claimed to feel for her, evaporate the instant she let him get too close? She was frightened of the answer.

Sara hardly slept that night. In the chill light of early dawn she looked at her reflection in the bathroom mirror and groaned. *After the way I treated Leo last night, he'll never want to see me again. Looking like this, he'd hardly recognize me, anyway.*

Unable to face breakfast, she showered and went straight out to the spa. Leo preferred his own company so he rarely used the place. That meant Sara could hide away all day there and recover without worrying. Their paths wouldn't need to cross until she felt strong enough to meet him.

She started with a swim. The pool's water didn't sting the wound on her leg as the sea had done. Floating in the crystal water made her feel more sleepy than during the whole of the previous night. That gave her an idea. An aromatherapy massage might help her wind down.

Half an hour later, Sara was lying facedown on one of the treatment beds. The therapist had mixed a soothing blend of rose, jasmine, and sweet almond oils. As she dozed, the woman worked over the tense muscles in her neck and shoulders. A soothing soundtrack of birds and a fountain was so much better than the clatter of keyboards.

Sara moved from dozing in the treatment room to dozing on a lounger in the shade of a spreading mulberry tree. The Paradise Spa was working its magic on her physically, but mentally she still couldn't rest. Her body, oiled and unwound, craved sleep. Her mind, still tormented by the way she had sabotaged her evening with Leo, played her over the surface of it like a fish. The soles of her feet grew warm as the sun moved around, but she couldn't be bothered to get up and move back into the shade as its power became stronger. It slid up to cover the backs of her legs, then her body. When it reached her shoulders a shadow fell across her, as though the sun had gone behind a storm cloud. She raised herself on her elbows and twisted around to see if the weather had changed.

The day was as bright as ever. That single shadow was cast by a familiar figure standing over her.

"You told me you weren't a lizard. I'm here to make sure you don't turn into one." He reached for the bottle of suntan lotion stowed beneath her lounger.

"Leo!"

"Lie still. I'll do your back first."

He was issuing orders again. First she roused, then she relaxed. This was kind, considerate Leo, after all. "Thank you. That's one thing I can't manage to do properly by myself."

"Everyone's got problems like that. Mine is not having the sense to quit while I'm ahead."

Sara hesitated. He didn't move until she obeyed. Stretching out facedown, she pillowed her head on her arms and closed her eyes. That made it easy to replace in her mind Leo's serious expression with the one she had seen so often on his face: the little lift at the corners of his mouth when he said something flirtatious.

The bottle sighed beneath the squeeze of his fingers. He lifted her hair away from her neck, and Sara found herself echoing the exhalation.

"This will be cold," he said.

"Not on a day like this—aah!" She flinched as he draped a trail of lotion around her neck. She bit her lip, anticipating his touch. He made her wait. She became painfully aware of the pulse throbbing beneath her skin, and he replaced the screw cap on the bottle with agonizing slowness.

Waiting for his touch was almost as delicious as her memories of him. "I was a fool last night, Leo."

"I know." All of the fun had returned to his voice, but none of the anger.

After another pause, she heard him move closer. She felt the change in temperature when his shadow eclipsed the sun. She held her breath, a current of anticipation running riot through her body as his presence drew nearer. When her fevered brain had almost conjured up his touch for herself, the bottle scraped as he dropped it onto the ground.

"Come on!" She groaned, hoping he didn't read the right meaning into her plea. Either way it was crude, but nothing like as crude as she felt. She wanted to get down and dirty with him right now, but this was the only danger-free way to get his hands in contact with her body.

"Very well. Who am I to argue with a lady?" Leo's voice rumbled with mock gravity. Then his hands swooped over her skin with the decisive movements of a man born to handle women. His first strokes ran straight up and down her back. He caressed the lotion into the hot skin of her shoulders using slow, circular movements.

"You've done this before."

"Once or twice."

"I can tell. You've honed your skill."

He clicked his tongue. "That's me! I'm the master of all those talents that don't really matter."

"Applying suntan lotion is important. It matters very much to me."

"You weren't so accepting of my touch last night."

His words spiked Sara's trance with an injection of reality. "You didn't do yourself any favours by coming on too fast, too soon."

"Stop acting the schoolmarm. It doesn't suit you. And I should point out I wasn't the one who asked for it 'fast and hard.'"

Sara grew hot at the memory, but Leo didn't tease her any more. His voice was low and seductive. "I've worked out what was behind last night. You wanted me on your own terms, and when I refused to play to your rules, you wouldn't compromise."

"It's called business."

"No. When a man spends an enjoyable evening with an attractive woman then wants to take it further, it's called romance."

Sara wanted to argue, but she didn't want to interrupt Leo. With glacial slowness she turned beneath his hands. He choreographed his movements with hers, leaning forward with a smile when the next sweep of his hand promised contact with her left breast. She raised herself on one elbow and his fingertips skimmed instead over the skin of her arm. His lips parted in a wolfish grin, showing those white, even teeth. He knew exactly what he was doing—and what she was doing too. She loved his teasing, for as long as she could keep her balance between wild desire and her need to stay in control.

"I've told you. I don't toy with my employees."

"I'm still employed by ACS, remember? Any working relationship has to be built on trust. If you're a rogue and likely to break your promises, I want to know."

He gave a lighthearted huff. "Aren't you already convinced you know the answer to that?"

"How can you be so sure what I think and feel?"

"Know your enemy." He gave her a lascivious look. "One of the first things I learned at medical school was the fastest way to a woman's heart. It's through her brain."

As he talked, his fingertips traced the curve of her inner arm. His eyes never left hers. They were mesmerizing. His touch moved ever closer to the smooth rise of her breast.

"And you think you're heading for my heart, do you?" As his fingertips began a delicate ascent of her breast, Sara's pulse hammered so hard through her body she knew he must be able to feel it.

"It's a little left of centre." His fingers glided in a sudden swoop over to her sternum.

"And as nearly-a-doctor, you're interested in that kind of detail."

"Absolutely fascinated." With his fingers resting on the spot, his palm brushed her nipple. The little bud hardened into a peak and pressed against his hand.

"It feels like you're interested too," he breathed, leaning forward as her lips parted. She didn't want to speak—he was tempting her with a delicious method of silencing her.

"Interested, but not insane, Mr. Gregoryan." Grabbing his hand, Sara moved it away. "This is why I haven't had a holiday in years. It melts through my good intentions and turns my brain to mush."

"That's the whole idea." He drew her into his arms and bent toward her for the kiss she couldn't resist any longer.

At the exact moment their lips met, their perfect solitude erupted. Krisia's voice rang out across the pool. "Leo! Thank goodness I've found you! Athan's on the phone—"

Sara groaned as Leo's expression glazed. He sat up. With a pang of resentment she saw his features morph back into his professional meet-and-greet face. She knew it meant nothing, but for an instant she had been entranced by being the centre of his total focus. It was haunting. She wanted to be bewitched again, right now, and Krisia was ruining it.

"I'll get rid of her." Leo leapt to his feet and called across the terrace. "Tell him to ring back, Krisia. I'm...in conference."

Sara had a split second of indecision. She needed to make Leo smile again, but experience had taught her pleasing a man at any cost was always a bad idea. Sara wanted Leo to turn her inside out with desire, but she had to see how he reacted before running her head into that particular noose a second time. Once tied, there was no easy way out.

"No, wait. Leave her to me." Sara stood up, her rangy athleticism in contrast to Krisia's generous curves. "Hi, Krisia. I owe you an apology. I shouldn't have had a go at you over your missing organizer. I was too tense. I definitely needed this holiday." She sashayed forward, giving Leo the full benefit of her walk away. Reaching out, she cupped the girl's shoulders to pull Krisia into a professional airkiss. The skin beneath her touch turned to goose flesh, and Sara's smile became genuine. "Leo and I were about to indulge in a bit of skinny dipping. Why don't you join us?" Her voice was a purr of undisguised desire.

Krisia blanched. "No—that's fine. I'll go and give Athan your message, Leo..." She backed away in confusion then hurried inside.

"That was brilliant," Leo said. "How did you manage it without upsetting her?"

"It was nothing," Sara wrinkled her nose and let one of her bikini straps fall. Leo stretched out a hand to lift it back in place, but she was already moving beyond his reach and toward the lounger. "As you say she's such a loyal employee, Krisia might have found the courage to strip off for you, though judging by her blushes I doubt it. She couldn't face shedding her clothes in front of a total stranger like me." She gave him an impish grin. "And now I have your undivided attention."

"You've got it, Gorgeous. And I'll make sure Krisia never bothers us again."

Sara wondered what that meant. When he mentioned his PA, it had been with a curl of his lip that looked like annoyance.

"You are still giving her that promotion though, aren't you?"

He replied so fast she knew he had it all worked out. "Of course. She's the efficient bookworm my feckless playboy of a brother needs. She'll soon whip him into line if he tries fooling about."

"It sounds like they'll drive each other mad."

"Probably...but he could do with the challenge. Somebody who'll stand up to him."

Without checking whether they were alone again, Leo swooped in and kissed Sara into oblivion.

"Wow...you don't mess about, do you?" She laughed, struggling to catch her breath.

"No, but I can always be persuaded to take my time. Like this..." He sipped another kiss from her lips. This time it was a slow, thoughtful encounter. "And I've got something far more luxurious than simple kisses planned for you." He drew his hands over her body.

"So why don't you let me in on the secret, Leo?"

"I'm waiting for you to dream up an objection.".

"Not this time. I'm too busy imagining what's in your mind."

"Then you'll raise no objection if I drag you off to my lair to enjoy you at my leisure?"

"Try it, and see."

"Hmm...maybe I'll have a little aperitif before my main course," he mused, kissing her again. This time his hands roamed over her body in an orgy of possession. As his fingers slid down over the taut warm curves of her rump he fondled her yielding flesh until she gasped with pleasure. That was his cue to slide his hands between the silky fabric of her bikini and the warm skin of her bottom. Sara threw back her head, exposing more skin to his kisses. As he moved his lips over her neck her body melted against him. As his hunger for her grew, he nipped at the delicate skin beneath her ears with increasing abandon.

"Do you know what I'd like to do to you?" he murmured in a voice like melted milk chocolate.

"Tell me...tell me..."

"I want to grab you, take you up to my suite, and make mad passionate love to you until all the stars go out."

Thrusting her hands into his hair she raised his head and kissed him, hard. "Don't talk. Do it."

Laughing, he swept her into his arms.

"So you've stopped being the independent woman who would rather walk?"

She pressed a finger to his nose. "No. But once in a while—a very long while—it's good to let someone else take control."

"You trust me to do that?"

"You've never given me any reason to doubt you. So far."

"And I never will." He breathed the words as he paced across the terrace and through the cool of the spa. As he leaned against the button of the lift there was time to revel again in the inspiration of a kiss.

Her eyes widened at the sight of their reflections in the mirrored walls of the elevator as he carried her in. "How many girls have you seduced like this, Leo?"

"Too many."

"Then I ought to say thank you, and good-bye."

"No. I want you, Sara, like I've never wanted any

other woman, and I'm a man who's experienced a lot of lust."

"That's quite a confession."

She expected him to laugh off her accusation, but he didn't. He concentrated on getting out of the lift with his precious burden, avoiding her gaze. "It needed to be made."

"No, it didn't. From the moment you surfaced in front of me out in the bay, I guessed what you were like, Leo Gregoryan."

"Once upon a time, maybe. Not any more. Not since I met you," he murmured.

He took her through the reception area of his suite and into his sunlit bedroom. It dazzled with the light off the sea and was filled with the fresh fragrances of flower arrangements and discreet furnishings.

"We must be quiet. My bodyguard sleeps in the next room"—he nodded toward a partition door—"and as we kept him up until all hours this morning, I said he could have a lie-in today."

"Did he follow us to the restaurant?"

"He tails me everywhere," Leo explained. "That deserves consideration so..." He put his finger to his lips for quiet.

An enormous bed stood on a platform at one end of the huge bedroom. Kicking off his shoes, Leo carried Sara to it and laid her on the rich surface. She sank into the thick, feather-filled field with a sigh of expectation.

"Seeing you stretched out like that makes me wish I'd brought the suntan lotion."

"You won't need it. I'm ready to slip through your fingers as it is."

"I'll have to see about that." He towered above her,

one foot on the floor, one knee on the edge of the bed. He was magnificent in his arousal, silhouetted against the bright white light of the window, and every inch the bronzed statue of a Greek god. She reached out to caress him.

"I thought you were only interested in power play, Sara."

"Not when the view from giving in is so good." Her eyes were drawn to an unmistakable outline pushing against the front of his trousers. As he slipped off his clothes, the percussion within her body became hammer blows of desire.

He looked incredible. Sara couldn't take her eyes off him. His naked body was lithe and flawless, with bronzed skin and exactly the right amount of dark body hair. She had admired plenty of men from a distance in her time, but Leo was right there for her. Every inch of his proud masculinity was on show. He was ready, willing, and she knew from sweet experience, perfectly able.

He was so self-assured he took her breath away. "I want you." He stopped. "If you want me too," he said, his voice a low caress of reassurance.

Sara nodded, but she couldn't move. To do that would make her complicit in whatever happened next, so if it all went wrong it would be her fault. Why should this Leo Gregoryan be any different?

"Because I love women, and I have nothing to prove," he said, and she realized she must have spoken her worries out loud. He wrapped his arms around her, bringing her in close to the sheltering security of his body. "We're here to enjoy ourselves, remember? The magic starts right now," he whispered, dipping his head to kiss her. "You do something to me, Sara. You're almost too hot to handle..." he murmured, his powerful hands cupping her face before his lips brushed hers again, testing her resolve.

She still meant to resist, but her body outwitted her brain. As though in a dream she moved beneath him, spreading her fingers over his shoulders. Her reaction inspired him. He took full possession of her mouth, robbing her of the will to resist. The tip of his tongue nudged hers.

She leaned into him, attracted to his irresistible force. This was the wrong time to wonder how many other women had been rendered senseless by his kisses, and manipulated by his strong, deft hands. Leo held her like some precious jewel. It was such a delicate restraint she could have broken away at any moment, but his hypnotic skill held her captive.

He slid the straps of her bikini over her shoulders, exposing the creamy skin beyond her tan lines. His seductive smile expanded as he enjoyed the view. Dipping his head, he nipped at her, seizing her nipple between his teeth. Testing it, teasing it he explored the margins between pleasure and pain. Her breasts throbbing with excitement, Sara squirmed beneath him. She could hear her own breathing, harsh above the hiss of the air-conditioning. The hammering of her heartbeat pleaded for release.

The moment he laid her on the bed, she wrapped her legs around his body, laying herself wide open to him. Tipping her hips brought her into intimate contact with the ridge of his masculinity as it pressed into her skin. Her excitement at the prospect of feeling him inside her, and losing control sent her mind spinning...

She opened her eyes. Leo was focussed on her face. In that instant she knew losing control was the last thing on this man's mind. He wanted her pleasure, and he could wait. His total domination sent rivers of fire coursing through her body. She shuddered with the power of it, and he moved like cool smoke to strip her naked. Despite the fire in his eyes he was so gentle, her body had never been so thoroughly appreciated.

Imagine coming home to this man every night, having all the time in the world to admire him and his techniques, in bed and out of it.

Then he drew his body over hers, giving them both the maximum sensation with the kiss of skin against skin. Holding her close, he trailed the tip of his tongue from the hollow of her throat to circle the areola of first one breast, then the other. As she reveled in the ecstasy he went on nibbling and licking all the way down her smooth, fragrant body. His hand ran along the inside of her thigh, parting her legs so he could kneel between them. The way he took pleasure in her body sent her blood running hot with expectation. The appreciation in his eyes told her he couldn't wait to make love to her. She reached for him, delighted they were both enjoying themselves. Their mutual lust acted like an aphrodisiac, pumping up every sensation until her whole body was alight. "I've never felt like this before, Leo."

"Then you haven't lived. I haven't even started yet..."

His hands moved over the warm planes of her hips, diving between her body and the bed to sample her willing curves. Instinctively she slid her legs around his waist, crossing her ankles to draw his body in closer contact with hers. Feeling his skin pressed against her was an excitement she could hardly bear. His growl of need told Sara her body would satisfy him. That enormous turn-on meant this was no longer about what he desired or what she wanted. It was about the two of them moving in harmony, melding their bodies in a dance of such sensual perfection, time stood still. She lost track of time as they entwined their bodies on the wide, sumptuous bed. Sex should be like this, every time. Two people pleasuring each other, with all the sensations flowing through their bodies in a closed circuit of delight.

Sara never dreamed things could get better. Then Leo rolled onto his back and drew her up the whole length of his body. Her thighs parted in a natural welcome, but she hesitated. "This is an unusual position for a guy who likes to keep women in their place. Are you sure?"

"I've never been more sure of anything in my life," he said. She rubbed her pursed lips provocatively against the thrusting head of him, making him push them open. His breathing became more ragged as she made him work for his pleasure. Arching his back, he eased himself into her with a moan of sheer pleasure. His hands went to her hair, twisting her thick locks between his fingers.

"This is going to be incredible." He breathed the words as she lowered herself farther. Every inch of his body tensed with the effort of restraining himself. She moved, riding him toward an earth-shattering orgasm. Their bodies found a perfect rhythm. She worked her hands over the smooth, muscular planes of his chest, delighting in the feel of his smooth skin. All the time his body rose and fell beneath her, lifting her to the heights then restraining her to make the moment last, but the feelings were too good and their movements too synchronized. He thrust deeper and faster. She fell forward, her riot of hair tumbling over his face. She moved her body to keep time with his until at last in an incredible expression of mutual orgasm they both cried aloud. At that moment, the sound of a door crashing open and a man's voice blew their intimacy wide open. She flung herself away, and faced the threat.

There was a stranger in the room. He was holding a gun.

A gun pointing straight at Sara's heart...

Chapter Twelve

"Madam...Your Majesty. I'm so sorry," the man said in broken English. He was as horrified as Sara. She grabbed a handful of bedclothes to cover herself. He raised his gun. It all happened so fast, the door separating Leo's suite from the bodyguard's room was still swinging on its hinges.

Leo spoke to the intruder in his own language, then tried to calm her. "Take no notice, Sara. He's seen it all before."

"He's never seen me like this before!" She was trembling, and trying to cover herself. The bodyguard was even more embarrassed. Stuffing his revolver into its holster, he backed out of the room the way he had come, and slammed the dividing door.

Leo sank back onto the bed. "I'm sorry about that. That's the trouble with being spontaneous. His lie-in, combined with our little tryst—"

Sara was furious. "How can you laugh at a time like this? How dare you put me through that!"

"It's all part of my life, I'm afraid."

The warm mist of Sara's satisfaction evaporated in the white heat of her anger. "That's not good enough. I've never been so ashamed in my life! Wait, what did he call you—Your Majesty? What was that about?"

"As I said. It comes with the territory. Quite literally."

Sara paused. "He meant it, then? You really are a king?"

Leo nodded, but admitting it made him uncomfortable. She felt that by the way he moved to envelop her in his arms and pull her back down onto the bed.

She stiffened, making it impossible for him. "What sort of king? Why didn't you tell me who you were?" Her voice was as shaky as her nerves.

"I am Leotric Gregoryanak, King of Kharova." His voice was thick and deep. "I assumed you knew, but were too softhearted to spoil my last few weeks of anonymity before I go back home and make everything official."

"No," she said. "That place again...and king... So that's why you spoke about your country."

"Yes. I'm uncrowned, but I'm still Kharova's ruler. You had no idea?" He sounded pleased he'd managed to keep his full identity from her for so long.

Sara wanted to cry, but the tears wouldn't come.

"If that's the case, my team and I must be doing something right. I loathe media intrusion, so my instructions are always to keep my public profile as low as possible," he said.

She twisted away. He started to follow her movements, but she tucked the sheet around her body. She was hiding from him like a stranger, while she tried to find her professional veneer again. "I understand that, Leo, believe me. I like to get on with my work without constant scrutiny. In my case it's by the management of ACS. When you're hounded by the media, it must be a million times worse. I can see how being followed everywhere would make a private man like you long for anonymity. But don't you see what you've done?"

"The only thing that matters to me is the fact I've seduced you." A smile danced in his eyes. Her expression wouldn't let it reach his lips.

She wrapped her arms around her body. It dawned on her she'd been dicing with disaster. "I didn't want to find a surrogate mother for your baby before I knew you were a king. Now I do know, along with all the other things I've heard about Kharova, I don't want anything to do with it. In a place like that it's probably treason. They'd kill you all."

"I've told you to forget it. I'm running out of inspiration. Matchmaking has kept my country united over the centuries. My suggestion was the safe, logical extension of that. My people are suspicious of foreigners, but I would insist a Kharovan bride and I remained childless. If I marry a foreign aristocrat, that would disappoint my people. A home-grown wife and a separately conceived child was my least-worst solution to all that."

"You never thought to tell me what you were, and why you were doing it?" Her voice was rough with disbelief.

"I assumed you knew, but were too decent and professional to make a big thing about it. You're no airhead."

Sara's mind ran back and picked up all the hints that had glided past her during their days together. She'd been too obsessed with her thoughts and feelings to read the signs. "No. I didn't."

He wasn't convinced. "The internet makes household names of everyone these days."

"I haven't been online since I arrived," she reminded him. A lot of the things Leo had said to her over the past few days were taking on a whole new meaning. "So the job you didn't want wasn't so much head of a family firm as ruler of—where exactly is Kharova? The ACS deal never got far enough for me to find out while I was in England."

"It's a small kingdom on the Adriatic. I'm king, and my brother Athan is in charge of the army," Leo said, with the sort of diffidence he might have used if they were running a local store rather than a country.

"Whenever you talked about your people, I assumed you meant the human resources team of your business. You meant the people of Kharova." She pieced clues together, warming to a conclusion. "And as for your talk about finding a surrogate mother...the more I think about it the worse it seems."

"My brother and I didn't agree about it, either."

"One of you must be talking sense, then. You can't go through with such an insane scheme, Leo! Not in a million years." Sliding out of bed, she gathered up her bikini.

"I don't see why not." He put his hands behind his head and watched her getting dressed. "There can't be much difference between organizing the future of a successful business, and a country."

Sara stopped, appalled. "I can see I'll have to say it again—you just don't get it, do you?"

"What's the problem? I thought you said it wasn't any of your business to judge what your clients wanted."

His words shocked Sara to the core. Was that all Leo supposed he was to her—a client?

"It isn't...but there's a big difference between securing a business empire and producing a royal family, a baby to order!"

"Is there?"

"Leo..." she gasped. "You aren't joking, are you?" Horror radiated from her.

"No."

"It's one thing to live with the threat of hostile financial takeovers. When you're talking about creating a life that'll need to be protected every second by security guards who burst into rooms armed to the teeth, that's something else entirely! I can't have a hand in bringing a baby into this world who's going to face that sort of threat every day of their life!"

"Fine. So I'll find someone else who can. Now come back to bed."

"You're not serious?" She stared at him, aghast. "You are, aren't you? How the hell can you lie there and say something outrageous like that?" The answer struck her before he had a chance to reply. Leo had inherited arrogance along with his royal pedigree. The descendant of powerful generations, he would never—could never—understand how anyone else felt about this. He would keep pushing at any problem until he got the result he wanted. To argue with him would be like trying to face down a hurricane.

Snapping the straps of her bikini into place, she stormed out of his suite.

After that, Sara stood on her balcony for a long time, full of regret. The fragrance of citrus and myrtle blossom rising from the gardens reminded her of those wonderful moments beside the pool, where Leo seduced her. He knew how to pleasure any woman, while she only wanted to please one man—him. It was such a fundamental difference between them it was heartbreaking. She couldn't go on staying at the Paradise Hotel after this. To risk bumping into him all the time, to know he was so close and yet out of reach would be impossible.

She smiled, thinking how he had been so attuned to her fear of getting behind the wheel of a car again. Then she remembered the mother and child they'd met in Athens. How they'd laughed at their mistakes, how generous he'd been and how natural it felt to hold baby Calista in her arms. Sara wondered how it would have felt to hold Leo's baby. That was at the heart of her dilemma. She'd spent the whole of her life needing to be part of a family. Now she had met the one man in the universe who could make all her dreams come true, but she had to abandon all thoughts of staying with him. For Leo to consider marrying without love showed how much he took his own family life for granted.

I have to turn my back on him now. Walk out, and never see him again.

That would be unendurable. She would keep her principles and her independence, but at a huge cost. It would mean spending the rest of her life worrying about how Leo had taken the news, how he would manage without her, and wondering what might have been. He'd never once said he loved her, but that didn't matter to her. At least he hadn't lied. Leo concealed the truth about things that hurt him, like the reason he abandoned his career. That was the extent of his deceit. He'd told her their fling could never be anything more than temporary. He hadn't made any empty promises.

Sara had to match that honesty. She couldn't

abandon him without saying good-bye. Screwing up all her courage, she dressed and packed her things.

Then she tucked plenty of tissues into her purse, and went to say good-bye to Leo forever.

The security man who had burst in on them let her into Leo's suite without a murmur. In the silence, Sara relived that awful moment in embarrassment.

She crept in, expecting Leo to be asleep. His bed was empty, its single satin sheet crumpled on the floor.

With a jolt, she saw the outline of his tall figure through the gossamer draped over the French doors leading to his balcony. He had pulled on some jeans, and was staring out over the view the same way she had done. Sara wondered what was going through his mind. She knew he must be thinking. Loving him had opened her eyes to all his endearing little habits, like jingling coins in his pockets when he was concentrating.

And yet he'd hidden the truth from her. Concentrating on that fact spurred her on. Words exploded from her, pain and accusation mixed up in one heartfelt cry. "I can't take all this, Leo!"

He whirled round, shocked.

"I thought I could, but I can't!" She clenched her fists and pressed them to her breasts. "I convinced myself a single night with you was all I wanted. I was wrong. With any normal man it could have turned into something more, but not with you. You're a king. I'm never going to be able to call you mine."

"Is that all?"

His matter-of-fact words knocked all the air out of her. Anguish turned to rage. "All? All? Isn't that enough?" Her fury was at fever pitch. "I've ruined everything by giving in to you. I've made a fool of myself again. Doesn't that mean anything to you?"

He stopped looking bemused, and swung into action. Striding forward, he grabbed her by the shoulders. "Sara, stop it. You mean the world to me. It doesn't have to be like this. Pretend you never found out who I am. Let it go."

Agony bubbled in her lungs. She gasped for air, dragging it into her body with the same urgency she still felt for his touch. "I can't do that. I'm no good at pretending. I've messed up, Leo. I've fallen in love with you, and that wasn't part of my plan. You were supposed to be nothing more than some fun in the sun, to make my time at the Paradise go faster."

"Sara?" His voice was no louder than a whisper, but there was a power about it that silenced her. "Sara? What did you say? I couldn't make sense of anything after you said—" He stopped.

"I said you were supposed to be some fun in the sun, that's all."

"No. Before that. What did you say before that?"

In her anguish, Sara twisted the tissue in her hands into a damp rope. She knew what he meant, but couldn't answer the question. The last time she said those dangerous words out loud to a man, it started a downward spiral into a horror of pain.

She mouthed the words, unable to give them body.

"I can't hear you," he said.

"This is all so new to me.."

"And me." His voice was barely louder than hers.

Sara had to blink hard. She was holding back tears, but felt her lips curve upward. Leo always had that effect on her. "What would you do if I said..." She faltered and stopped. The shreds of tissue dropped to the floor like melting snow. "D'you know, I don't think I can say it again." She gave a watery laugh.

"Then let me say it first." He took her hands in his. "I love you, Sara Astley."

His honesty reverberated through her whole body and Sara found blinking wasn't enough any more. Her tears fell at the same moment she threw herself into his arms. "But I've made such a mess of my life!"

"Don't knock it. Every moment has brought us closer to this one." His voice was rough with emotion as he buried his face in her hair and held her so close she could hardly breathe.

"Yes...but it can't last." She had to speak, and fought to free her mouth from his kisses. "You need a queen, not a businesswoman!"

"I don't need either of those things. I want you."

His words twisted her heart. "Why couldn't you have told me you were the king? I would never have come within a million miles of you! I love you more than I ever thought possible, and now I have to let you go. Why can't you make it up somehow with Mihail? Let him have Kharova. He can put up with that horrible country's ridiculous rules, instead of you."

She pushed her face into the curve of his neck, trying to stifle her sobs. As he held her, she felt his chest expand as he drew in a huge breath.

"That's a wonderful idea, but I can't. Mihail has a lot of vocal support, but there's not much actual power behind him. If I hand the crown over to him, it will cause more problems than it solves. But I want you to know you're the first woman I've ever come close to obeying, Sara."

Resting her hands on his shoulders, she leaned

back in his arms. She had never seen him look so irresistible. "Then can I ask you to do something for me, Leo?"

"I'm yours to command. You'll always be queen in my heart," he murmured.

"Make love to me. Make love to me like it was the first time, not the last time, and we were going to be together forever."

"That would give me the greatest pleasure of my life, my love," he whispered.

His lips were cool and firm as always, but this time there was none of his usual rapid insistence. Instead, he cradled her to his body and kissed her until she forgot everything but his gentle caresses. Lifting her into his arms, he smiled with pride. "Do you remember the first time I did this?"

"I'll never forget. I was so hot for your body, but so angry at the way you'd dived into my life and started ordering me around."

"And now, as I say, I'm yours to command." He sighed the words between kisses and carried her to the bed. Sara's body turned to liquid honey beneath his hands, soft and golden.

Leo had made love many times, but until now he had never loved. There had been too many other women, if he was honest. And he intended to be honest with Sara from now on, however long or short their time together might be.

Chapter Thirteen

Their lovemaking was seductive and slow as they took pleasure in exploring and pleasuring for the last time. Sara had never felt loved before she met Leo. Now she felt adored. He was an incredible lover, gentle and appreciative of her body in so many ways. His body slid over hers in a dance that swept them both to the heights of passion.

Afterward, they lay together in a peace disturbed by the sands of time trickling away from them.

"I must go," she said, but made no move to lift her head from his chest.

"Stay."

They both knew he meant forever. She shook her head. "I have to let you go, Leo. My bags are packed and down in the reception area. The taxi will be here soon."

"I could forbid you to leave. I am a king, after all."

His smile was sad and sweet. She rose, running her hands over his chest and down his arms, reluctant to lose the feel of his skin beneath her fingers until the last moment. "You could, but you won't." She kissed his brow, then pressed her forehead against his.

"There will be a place of honor reserved for you at my coronation, Sara."

"Don't expect me to leap up and object during the ceremony, as if it was a wedding." She tried to smile. "I know you'll make a brilliant king."

"I'd make a better lover for you, than I would make a king."

"You can't afford to think like that. Make some penniless principality rich beyond its wildest dreams by marrying its blue-blooded princess, and producing dozens of healthy sons and daughters."

He grabbed her again. "Don't joke about it. While I am king and Mihail is a threat to my country, the situation is too grave for humour."

Sara remembered something, and drew herself from his arms. "Why not persuade your brother to marry and produce a legitimate child? He sounds like he could whip the locals into shape with one hand, while beating back your cousin Mihail with the other."

Leo made a gesture of exasperation. "Athan? Marry? I wish. That'll never happen. He's having too much fun playing around."

"Like us."

Sara would remember all the good times with Leo for the rest of her life. His touch would haunt her forever, but she forced herself to pull away from him.

Leo had no intention of letting her go so easily. He followed her into the shower, ignoring her halfhearted attempts to send him away. "I want to spend every last second with you."

He made sure she could never doubt it. Dry, she was irresistible. Svelte and slippery with shower gel, she was his for the taking. He ravished her beneath the warm rain of the shower until she cried his name with such longing he buried his face in her hair as his emotions overwhelmed him.

Sara...oh, Sara, how am I going to live without

you? When she reached for the shower button he stayed her hand while the flow of water washed away the grit suddenly filling his eyes at the thought of losing her.

"I will never stop wanting you," he said later, as he wrapped her in a huge, soft towel. Pressing its fluffy folds against her skin he dabbed her dry, taking his time to memorize every part of her beautiful, wanton body.

"And you will fill all my fantasies until the end of time."

When she whispered that, he felt strips tear away from his heart, leaving it raw and irreparable.

Sara tugged herself from his grasp. "I must get ready for the taxi. It'll be here any minute."

I must be mad, she thought, walking out on a man who says he loves me, and makes no secret of the fact I'm at the centre of his universe. "I'll never endure a long good-bye, so I'll go down to the foyer and wait on my own. I don't want you hanging around in a public place. Now I know who you are, I'm afraid other people will discover your secret too. If that happens, you might not be safe here for much longer, Leo."

"That's not what matters. All I care about is you, my love."

His gruff reply was another direct hit on Sara's heart. When she arrived at the Paradise Hotel, her heart and soul had been too battered to risk giving any man— even Leo—the excuse to start ordering her life for her. She would remember him as a kind and sensitive lover. She wanted to believe he wouldn't have tried to take over her life. As long as she was in control, no man could ever hurt her again. Not even if that man was Leo.

"I believe you." How many times would she have

to say those words before she could accept them as true? "That's why I have to get out of the picture and leave you free to concentrate on your life in Kharova."

She checked her watch again. "My plane leaves at three. The taxi should have arrived by now. I wonder where it's got to." She tapped the numbers of the taxi firm into her phone, but the sight of Leo pulling on his clothes was too much of a distraction. She was only half listening to the booking clerk, but the news was bad enough. "They don't know what's happened to it, and there's no time to get another car out here from the depot." She frowned. "I hope he's okay."

"Give me the taxi firm's number, and I'll check up on him again for you once I've seen you onto your flight." Tousled and barefoot, Leo padded around the room searching for his keys and the socks he had scattered on their way to bed. He looked so normal it was impossible to imagine he was the same man who could turn into an aloof monarch if his superiority was challenged.

"Are you offering to give me a lift?"

"It'll mean we have more time together. Every moment with you will give me a million memories."

"What about your bodyguard? I thought you'd given him the day off."

"I'm sure he can look after himself until I get back."

"You can't abandon your security! They're supposed to keep you safe!" she said, but the thought of making their time together last a little bit longer was a powerful argument.

"It'll be fine for an hour or so," he said. "Trust me."

They walked down the stairs in silence. Their minds were too full to speak. Leo tried to make conversation, but Sara couldn't trust herself to join in. She had to get away, but wanted to take him with her, to somewhere safe where the rest of the world would never find them.

Leo gave the security guard a nod as he guided his sleek blue car through the hotel's gates. Then he tensed, alert to a shape heading down the open road toward them.

"That must be your taxi trying to make up for lost time. Do you want me to stop him so he hasn't had a wasted journey?" he said.

"It doesn't matter," Sara muttered, too sad to care. Something wasn't quite right about the way it was taking such a direct line along the narrow country lane, but she couldn't find it in her heart to bother. "I left the fare and a decent tip with your bodyguard. The driver won't miss out."

"I love the way you've pinned your hair today. Almost as much as I love you." He revved the engine.

She glowed at the compliment, but shrugged it off. "If I'm going to be whisked along in this babe-magnet of yours, I don't want my hair getting all tangled. And you'd better watch what that maniac in the taxi is doing rather than look at me, Leo Gregoryan."

"Don't worry. I'll wait for him to turn in here before I pull out—"

He never finished. The taxi didn't intend pulling into the grounds of the Paradise Hotel. It headed straight for them, like a guided missile. Leo stamped on the accelerator, throwing the car forward in a desperate attempt to dodge out of the way. As the vehicle plowed into the side of their vehicle, Sara recognized the driver.

It was the man who had picked up Krisia's organizer from the terrace.

In a moment of total stillness everything went black. Sara couldn't think where she was, and why day had turned into night. Then any number of alarms burst into life, and she found herself lying on the hard tarmac. The rich upholstery of Leo's car lay fragmented around her. A vibration beneath her body brought her wading back to full consciousness, or as close to it as she could get. She realized the sensation was the pounding beat of running feet, and called, "Leo!"

The cloud of dust filling her lungs muffled her voice. She cried out, reaching for the hand that had been holding hers just minutes before. All the terror she felt when her own car went off the road rushed back, but this time there had been no lucky escape. She had woken to a reality as dark as her nightmares. Sara curled into a protective ball. Pain circled like a shark, haunting the shadows surrounding her. She fought the darkness, but it was too powerful. The next wave sucked her under. She closed her eyes, and with one last word almost slipped into unconsciousness. "Leo..."

The air was thick; she could hardly breathe. Fingers made contact with her neck. She forced her eyes open again. "Leo! Oh, thank God you're alive!"

He was covered in dust and streaked with blood. "What happened? What happened to you?"

"Shhh, my love. Don't try to speak."

"But your face!" She tried to wipe it clean with the back of her hand

"I'm fine," he said, his voice muffled as he caught

her wrist. Frowning at his watch, he concentrated on her fluttering pulse.

"My ears are full of cotton wool." She shook her head, but the feeling wouldn't go away.

"That taxi was aimed straight at us. I must have been the target. Luckily my car's modified to withstand most kinds of attack. The rescue services are on their way. We'll get you to hospital."

He sounded calm, but for the first time since they met, she saw uncertainty in his eyes. "Leo, listen...there's something I've got to tell you."

He touched her lips with one finger. "Not now. This is all my fault, Sara. I am so sorry. I knew getting close to you would put your life in danger. That's why I tried to resist, but it was impossible." He spoke in an undertone.

She had to fight to hear what he was saying, and she was frightened by what it might mean. Things must be bad for her. That settled it. She couldn't die without telling him the truth. "I don't care about the danger. All I want is you." She hesitated, then as he stroked her hair back from her brow she felt a surge of certainty. "Forever."

He froze. "Are you sure?"

She scrubbed at her face with one fist. Her head ached and her ears were still fuzzy, and she felt so tired. All she wanted to do was close her eyes and go to sleep.

He caught her hand and pulled it away. "Stop it. Sara, stay awake. Tell me again."

"Want you forever...but your duty...Kharova..."

"To hell with duty! Sara, you have to know I won't abandon you. Not now, not ever! This"—he gestured to the twisted wreckage beside them—"this is the reason why we had to part. I never wanted to inflict it on you!"

"You didn't. It was him. It was that man I told you about. The one who picked up Krisia's organizer," she mumbled.

"That does it. I'm never leaving you again. Not for a second," he whispered, and gave her a kiss to cushion her against the sirens, and sudden confusion of voices and people milling around them.

"I've got such a pain in my shoulder," she grumbled as the crash team lifted her onto a gurney.

"I've got the perfect cure for that. If a kiss can waken a fairytale princess I'm sure I can use one to distract my own leading lady."

"Is that what the doctor ordered?" She smiled, hoping it was.

"Yes. And I'll keep kissing you all the way to the hospital."

"I thought only next of kin could travel in ambulances."

"I'm sure I can persuade them to let me in on a technicality."

"You mean you're going to pull rank as King of Kharova?" She tried to look scornful, but the effort was too much. As a medic found a vein to put in a line, she drifted away.

Leo stared out the window. The hospital provided everything a king might need and more, from TV to champagne, but they might as well not have bothered. All he could think about was Sara. From the moment his eldest brother died, Leo had kept his mind trained on one thing. "Trained" was the right word. Putting Kharova before everything else wasn't an instinctive duty. Other people spent their lives trying to get out of uncomfortable situations. Loyalty always pulled Leo in the opposite direction. Instead of finishing his medical training and working to save lives, he'd taken up a role that meant living in the shadow of danger for the rest of his life. He could have stood that. It was the threat to those around him he couldn't stomach. Duty had brought him a long way, and this was how it repaid him.

Sara was still in surgery.

The events of that day had brought Leo to the end of the line. Weighed against the life of the woman he loved, generations of tradition looked as light as feathers.

Reaching for his mobile, he stabbed out a number and paced up and down the room while the phone connected. "Leo? They said you're not badly hurt. Is that true?" Athan's worried voice answered.

"I'll survive. What's the latest? Have you found out any more about who did it?"

"The driver? Yes. His body was pretty well smashed up. He hadn't bothered with a seatbelt, and there was no airbag. Your bodyguard found his wallet. Turns out he was a clansman of Mihail with more money than sense, trying to impress the rebels."

"Mihail—so this is his doing?" he groaned.

"Hold on, Leo. I haven't finished. The guy was a loose cannon, acting on his own because no one else trusted him. I've been on to Mihail, and I'm convinced he didn't know anything about this.'

"Do you believe him?"

"When I told him who it was, he was incandescent. I've known Mihail since school, don't forget, and he can't fake innocence. He agreed with me. An attack like this brings shame on our whole country," Athan said. "Right now, I'd say Mihail feels as much horror over what happened to you, as anyone else in our country does."

Leo felt some of the tension in his body ease. "That's good, but can Mihail deflect all the lunatics who want to make names for themselves?"

"No, of course not. That's why you have bodyguards. Even then, they can't stop the determined nutcase."

"So that's my life from now on? Waiting for the next maniac to have a go at me?"

"You've always known that, Leo. What's the matter?" Athan sounded concerned. "I've never known you to be scared of anything before."

"I'm not scared…not for myself. You know me better than that. But I won't allow people I love to be put through hell like this."

"Worry about that when it happens. It's not as if you've got a family yet."

Leo hesitated. "Not yet, no."

"Ah…Krisia mentioned you're interested in a new piece of crackling. That was the woman in the car with you, was it?"

"Don't believe everything Krisia says. She's had the knives out for Sara ever since they first met."

"Actually, Krisia's cooled about that. I get the impression she thinks you could do worse. At a pinch."

Leo relaxed even more. Bringing Sara into the conversation was helping him to reach a decision. It was one he'd never dreamed he would make. "That's a backhanded compliment, but better than nothing I suppose." He felt calm enough to risk a joke. "You and

Krisia getting on all right, are you?"

"We'll drive each other mad, but I've got to admit she's very good at her job. You can't have her back, if that's what you're angling for."

"No, she's better off where she is. But listen—I want to ask you something. Something important, so I need you to think hard about it, and not rush into anything."

"I'm listening." Athan's reply was guarded.

"What if I didn't want to be king?"

"You can't not be king." Athan sounded puzzled. "You're the heir. It's like saying you want to give up breathing."

"Of course it isn't, and there are far more important things in life than titles and traditions. I wanted to change a lot of those traditions anyway, so why not start with this one? I'm turning down the job.

Athan's voice was barely a whisper. "Leo? You can't be serious."

"I've never been more serious about anything in my life. If I was alone in the world, I'd buckle down and get on with it, but I've got Sara to consider now. Why can't you take my place on the throne? We both know you'd make a better king than I would, and you've got no intention of falling in love."

"Too right!" Athan snorted.

"Also, Mihail likes you more than he likes me."

"Dislikes me less than he loathes you, you mean."

"Whatever. He's less likely to cause trouble if you're king. You could even marry into his clan. You suggested it to me, and I know you don't have a problem with purely political liaisons. That way, everyone would be happy," Leo said, and heard Athan hum over the idea.

"The traditionalists would kick."

"There'll always be some people ready to make a fuss, whatever happens. While I'm king they'll be vocal about it, which encourages rebellion. If you're king, anyone who disagrees with what you say or do will have to either forget it or fight, because that's the way you work, Athan. I'm not like that. I want everyone to be happy, all the time. That's not possible. "

"So…if I did agree to become king," his brother said, with a cautious show of interest in the idea, "what would be left for you to do?"

"Whatever you, as the new King of Kharova, want. As long as my future wife and children are never at risk."

There was a long silence. So much depended on Athan's reaction. Whatever happened, Leo was determined to give up the crown, but he wanted the transition to be as painless as possible.

"All right," Athan said at last. "If you do decide to abdicate, I'll try to be as good a king as you would have been."

When Sara awoke, Leo was sitting beside her. For long moments she let herself revel in his smile. It was enough to know he was safe.

"Did you have to bully the emergency services into giving you a lift in the ambulance?" she said before spotting the blue sling cradling his left arm.

"No. A busted collarbone won me the sympathy vote."

She gave an anguished cry. "Oh, Leo—you must be in agony!"

"I'll heal. I'm more concerned about you. How do

you feel? Shall I call a nurse?"

She shook her head. "You're all I need."

"And to think... I might have lost you."

She went pale, and Leo grabbed her hand to reassure her. "I mean, I was almost too slow to stop you leaving me."

"Now you're worrying me!"

He lifted her hand to his lips and kissed each finger as she curled them around his.

"They've had to pin your shoulder, and you've got a few nasty bumps and bruises, but you'll be fine. They'll be keeping you in for a few days, so I've made sure you've got the best room in the house." He smiled at her. "That makes you my captive audience. I let you slip through my fingers once, Sara. That's not going to happen again."

"Oh...but we've been through all this, Leo. As King of Kharova, you can't marry a commoner like me, and I won't settle for anything less than marriage. That's the end of it."

"No, it isn't. Our stupid argument has got to stop. If you hadn't wanted to leave me, you wouldn't have been traveling in my car."

Sara wasn't letting him get away with that. "Please don't try and twist everything I do and say against me."

"You didn't let me finish. Your life was saved by the security systems that surround me, but they're only necessary in the first place because of my job."

"It's not a job. You were born to rule."

"That's the whole point—I wasn't. My brother Zacari was!" Letting go of her he pushed his hand through his hair in exasperation. "He was trained for the role from birth. Succeeding to the throne was the last thing I expected. I wasn't trained for it. I never wanted to be king."

Sara hesitated before answering back.

"You'll change."

"I came to the throne by accident." His voice was rough and hesitant.

"And I never wanted to fall in love again...until I met you. That was an accident too." She smiled. "It makes quite a change to be ruled by fate for once."

"Sara? Are you speaking for both of us?" he asked.

"I don't know. Am I?"

He jerked his head in the smallest nod. Taking her good hand, he leaned forward until his brow was touching hers. It felt so natural and wonderful that tears sprang into her eyes.

"Good...but that feeling might pass," she forced out in a whisper.

His face fell, dragging her heart down with it. She couldn't bear to wreck his happiness.

"We have to face facts. Leo, I want you in my life more than I've ever wanted promotion or honors or wealth or fame. But I don't want to live in fear of this happening again, to either of us!" She didn't want to let him go, so she moved in his grasp to point out the bruises staining her damaged arm.

His expression hardened. "You don't need to."

"I'd worry every second about the threat to your life, and...and to our children." There. The certainty was growing inside her that she wanted to marry Leo and carry his baby. Nothing else would do. Now she had said it out loud. She drew in a deep breath that shuddered over all the obstacles ahead.

"Marry me."

As his words sank in, she switched her attention straight back to him. "What?"

"Marry me. Then I'll make sure no one comes within a mile of my beautiful, adorable wife. "

A month ago she would have been horrified at the suggestion. Now all she wanted was Leo, but the man—not the king.

"I'm sorry. I am so, so sorry...but I have to say no, my love," she whispered through a sudden rush of tears.

He was aghast. "How can you call me your love, yet still refuse to marry me?"

"It's not you. It's your destiny. You're the rightful King of Kharova. You've said it often enough. But for as long as you're king, we can't marry. It's all that could persuade me to abandon you, and nothing's changed."

He eased his hand from her grasp and slid it over the coverlet.

"When we met, my country was my life. But you, and the children that will grow from our love, that's my concern now. It's why I've decided to make a stand, and pass the crown of Kharova on to Athan. Subject, of course, to your agreement."

A tense silence fell, enveloping them. Sara hesitated for a long time before breaking through it. "Leo? You'd do that for me?" she whispered.

"Of course. There's no contest. I want to be a wholehearted husband, not a halfhearted monarch. I'm stepping down so I can support you in the career you love. It's the perfect solution."

"What about your brother? You said Athan didn't want the job."

"That's because he has the same old-fashioned

views I had about inheritance, before I met you. I'm the elder brother, so in his eyes, that meant the crown was mine. It's no way to choose the best man for the job—which happens to be Athan. I'm a diplomat. He's the warrior our people need. He'll keep them safe. Everyone knows Athan would make a brilliant ruler of Kharova. The trouble is that with the exception of Mihail and his merry men, the whole of Kharova is too hobbled by tradition to tell me to my face."

"What a place." Sara shook her head in wonder.

"You'll love it. He drew her into his arms and gave her a sweet, lingering kiss. "You'll always be the queen of my heart, but will you mind not being Queen of Kharova, my love? The final decision is yours."

"I want what you want." She looked up at him as she lay in his arms. "Which reminds me. What about the other love of your life, nearly-a-doctor Gregoryan? A super-intelligent guy like you will need something more to do than be my partner at corporate functions. Why don't you go back to medical school, and finish your degree? Then later on, I'll stay at home and look after our baby, while you go out to work."

He smiled, but she saw him hitch a tiny breath. "And let you have all the fun? No way. We'll job-share."

Sara wanted a real life. Leo was the man to give it to her—but she still had one concern. "What happens if our first baby grows up with a burning desire to be ruler in their own land, and thinks we've denied them?"

"We'll worry about that if it happens," Leo said. "For now, I can't see Athan getting married any time soon. He'll be no more keen to put a child through what we've suffered than I am. For the moment anyway, I'm leaving the matter of the succession up to him. I'll be too busy enjoying myself with you. You are perfection, my love, and all I want is the chance to hold you in my arms whenever I like, for as long as I like."

The time for words had passed. Leo's hand went to the back of Sara's head, cradling it as he kissed her. At the touch of his lips she felt herself melting all over again. As he molded her battered body to the powerful contours of his own, she knew they would never be parted again.

A word about the author...

Christina Hollis lives deep in the English countryside. She met her husband on a blind date, and during a career break to raise their family she wrote a lot of short stories. It's an activity that fits in well with parenting timetables. Her writing grew into a full-time career in romantic fiction, and her books have appeared in lists of best-sellers all over the world.

~*~

www.christinahollis.com

Thank you for purchasing
this publication of The Wild Rose Press, Inc.

If you enjoyed the story, we would appreciate your
letting others know by leaving a review.

For other wonderful stories,
please visit our on-line bookstore at
www.thewildrosepress.com.

For questions or more information
contact us at
info@thewildrosepress.com.

The Wild Rose Press, Inc.
www.thewildrosepress.com

Stay current with The Wild Rose Press, Inc.

Like us on Facebook

https://www.facebook.com/TheWildRosePress

And Follow us on Twitter
https://twitter.com/WildRosePress